THE TEA SHOP

BERNADETTE MARIE

5 PRINCE PUBLISHING

THE TEA SHOP

Bernadette Marie

5 PRINCE PUBLISHING & BOOKS, LLC

PO Box 16507

Denver, CO 80216

www.5PrinceBooks.com

Digital ISBN-13: 978-1-63112-213-2

Print ISBN-13:978-1-63112-214-9

THE TEA SHOP. Bernadette Marie

Copyright Bernadette Marie 2018

Published by 5 Prince Publishing

Cover Credit: Tilted Tiara Designs

First Edition 2018

To Stan,
I saw you in my dreams and you appeared.
I love you forever and a day!

ACKNOWLEDGMENTS

To my dream man: Thank you for always believing in all the strange and weird things I see!

To those I dreamed of: Being your mom is the greatest dream come true.

To my dream family: I'm lucky to have been raised in a house with love and compassion.

To my dream team: So you all left me for Australia and Brazil. Still love that you keep me grounded and focused on what I love to do.

To my dream readers: You make me want to continue to dream up new and exciting stories.

To the little boy in the footed PJs: I think of you.

Finding Hope

THE THREE MRS. MONROES TRILOGY

Amelia

Penelope

Vivian

THE ASPEN CREEK SERIES

First Kiss

Unexpected Admirer

On Thin Ice

Indomitable Spirit

THE DENVER BRIDE SERIES

Cart Before the Horse

Never Saw it Coming

Candy Kisses

ROMANTIC SUSPENSE by BERNADETTE MARIE

Chasing Shadows

THE TEA SHOP

Bernadette Marie

CHAPTER 1

"Carson, this is absolutely delightful." Ellie Winters placed her napkin in her lap as she looked around the quaint tea shop. "This is exactly what this town needed," she said. "It's gotten filled up with sock stores and fancy eating places that I don't want to go to. Tea shops with linens is a nice nod to the way things used to be."

Carson chuckled at Mrs. Winters as he crossed one leg over the other and took in the view himself. It was quaint and cute. He was sorry, though, to hear she didn't like the fancy eating places that were popping up. Perhaps in their past outings, she'd missed the part where he'd let her know he was an investor in three of them.

What did it matter really? Ellie Winters was eighty-two years old and Carson certainly valued her opinion of the town where she'd raised her family.

Conversation halted when the woman who had seated them came back to the table with a tray holding a silver teapot that steamed, two dainty antique teacups, and a few other items he was sure she was going to explain to them.

She, Carson thought, was as cute as the quaint cafe Mrs.

1

Winters was taken with. He watched as she set the antique cups and saucers in front of them and explained the pattern, of all things.

"These cups are RS Prussian. They date back to 1869," she said as she added a silver spoon to each of their settings. Next, she set down a plate as dainty as the cups between them, with two strange contraptions. "These are your tea strainers."

With an open hand, and not pointing with her finger, she gestured to the one closest to Mrs. Winters. "You chose peppermint tea." Then she gestured to the other and looked at him as she spoke. "And you, Earl Grey."

He gave her a slow nod as she set another bowl on the table. "Sugar cubes for your tea, and of course, cream," she offered as she set the small pitcher on the table between them. "I'll have your sandwiches right out."

The woman turned and walked away, and Carson noted that Mrs. Winters smiled after her.

"She is delightful," she said as she turned back to the table. "This is beautiful. Carson, I do enjoy our afternoons."

"I do too. You let me know where you want to go next and I'll get that set up as well. If I'm not mistaken, you have a birthday next month. Where would you like to celebrate?"

Her cheeks pinked, and that brought him joy. She might be edging into eighty-three, but she soaked up life—every minute of it.

"Let's see how this goes. They have a dessert tray we didn't order. Maybe we can have that next month."

How could he not agree to that? His monthly outings with Ellie Winters brought him as much joy as they did her. And wouldn't it be nice to take in the view again, he thought as the woman came back to the table with a tower of plates delicately stacked with sandwiches and little cakes.

She expertly arranged the table so that the tower would sit between them. Again with her open hand, she gestured. "We have an array of delightful sandwiches and cakes for you today. Here we have a cucumber sandwich, egg salad on rye, and my favorite; a goat cheese, walnut, and roasted pepper sandwich."

Mrs. Winters' eyes opened wide, and Carson was sure she swooned.

"Oh, now doesn't that sound delightful, Carson?"

"Positively," he said, looking up at the waitress who caught his eye then quickly diverted her attention back to the tray.

The woman swallowed hard, then licked her lips, which had his stomach tightening.

"For the desserts we have eclairs, a delightful lemon tart, and raspberry and dark chocolate tarts. Then, of course, we have scones on the bottom plate, and your clotted cream is on the table."

Mrs. Winters placed her hand on her chest. "My, this is a lot."

The woman smiled. "I'm happy to box up any leftovers you might have. They'll make for a wonderful tea tomorrow afternoon as well."

"That sounds perfect," Mrs. Winters agreed.

"Let me know if I can get you anything else," she said with a smile.

Carson eased back in his seat again. "What is your name?" he asked, and watched as her eyes went wide.

"Abigail."

"This is your store, isn't it?"

Her cheeks filled with color, not out of embarrassment, but certainly out of pride. "Yes. We opened a few months ago. It's only myself and my cousin, Clare, at the moment. We make everything right here. We also arrange for high tea to go, if you're ever in need," she'd offered as she turned her attention to Mrs. Winters who had reached her hand out and touched Abigail's arm.

"You're going to do well here, my dear. I should know. I've lived around here for eighty-two years. Almost eighty-three." She

3

laughed that warm laugh that always brought a warmth to Carson's soul. "I'll tell everyone I know."

"I appreciate that." He noticed the shake in her voice, and her lips that trembled as they tried to smile. "Are you celebrating today?" Abigail asked.

Carson shook his head. "I take this beautiful woman out to lunch each month, and have for ten years now."

Mrs. Winters reached her hand across the table and patted his, as she often did. "He takes good care of me."

Carson noticed Abigail's smile fade, but only briefly before she forced it back to her lips. "I'll let you two enjoy your tea. Please let me know if I can bring you anything else."

He watched as she walked away, and then was drawn back to his guest when she slapped his hand. "Don't you go looking at her like that," Mrs. Winters said as she pulled an egg sandwich from the tray and set it on her plate. "She's a nice girl."

Carson uncrossed his legs and moved in to take a cucumber sandwich for himself. "Now why do you say it as if I shouldn't be interested in a nice girl?"

Mrs. Winters brushed her hand through the air. Her bracelets jingled, and her many rings caught the light. "You should be interested in them. And you should marry yourself one. I saw that last woman you dated," she warned, holding up a finger. "Oh, Carson, she was nothing but trouble looking for a good time."

Yes, she was, he thought to himself as he took his first bite of the delectable little sandwich. Susanna Morris was high mainte-nance, and he'd lost interest quite quickly. She, on the other hand, nearly had them married. The very thought made him sweat under his collar. Carson came from a well-off family, and he'd had his own financial success. He invested in businesses he thought would increase his portfolio nicely, and they had. Then there was the matter of his little dot-com business, which he'd started in college, and it had been bought out by a bigger dot-com. That had seeded what had become a fortune of his own.

Though he enjoyed lavish things, nice vacations, and spoiling a certain old woman, his mind hadn't gone to marrying anyone. Perhaps he was afraid they would want him for the wrong reasons. That's why he'd gone into real estate developing. Not only did it fulfill his passion for building things, but it also kept him much too busy to go searching for a woman.

Movement at the counter caught his eye, and he watched as Abigail helped a customer who had walked in and then served another table.

There was something about her that had his mind wandering to places it shouldn't be. Her dirty blonde hair was pulled back in a ponytail. She'd had little, if any makeup on at all. The simple cotton dress she wore beneath her frilly apron wasn't designer, and neither were the flat shoes she wore to work in. But when those crystal blue eyes had looked at him, he was sure there had been some kind of jolt that zapped his chest. He'd never been into her quaint little store, she wasn't his type, but he couldn't help but think that he'd seen the woman before.

"Drink your tea," Mrs. Winters scolded. "It's going to get cold while you watch her work."

He chuckled. "I'm not watching her work."

"Hmmm," she made the noise at him as any grandmother would to a grandchild. "I think I would like to have lunch here for my birthday next month. Make sure to make reservations before we leave."

"I will do that," he said as he sipped his perfectly sugared tea. "Which cake is your favorite? I'll get you a box to take home as well."

"You're too good to me, Carson." She smiled brightly. "I like the lemon one."

CHAPTER 2

*A*bigail watched from the kitchen as the man and the older woman left the store. They had boxed up the left-over sandwiches and scones from their tea, and then he'd ordered her a box of lemon cakes to take home.

It had delighted Abigail that the woman had fussed over the box, tied with ribbon. That was exactly the kind of reaction she wanted from her customers. Everything they sold was wrapped up like a special gift. After all, why buy something you liked if it didn't feel just like that—a gift.

The tip the man had left her was more than generous. Part of her had thought to chase after him and refuse it. After all, it was nearly as much as the total tea and extra cakes. She was sure he could afford it. The custom-made suit, polished shoes, and diamond encrusted face on his watch would have told anyone he was well-off. Not to mention the nicely-groomed haircut which had certainly caught her eye when he'd looked up at her with those dark, chocolate eyes.

Though she didn't get the impression he looked the way he did to flaunt his money. She assumed he liked fine things—and he could afford them. It also made a nice package to look at, she mused to herself. Hopefully, he hadn't noticed that she'd indulged in such a thing as looking at him while he had his tea with his companion.

"Hey, you okay?" Clare nudged her out of her trance. She'd gone on too long watching the man walk the woman to the black Audi and help her inside before walking around the car to the other side and climbing in himself.

"Yeah, I'm fine." She turned and rinsed the dishes off in the sink before putting them in the dishwasher.

"He's a fine looking man," Clare looked out the window, then went back to making the egg salad for tomorrow's lunch.

"Who? Oh, the customer with his grandmother?"

"Yeah, him. And are you sure it wasn't his date?" Clare humored.

Abigail shook her head. "No, I don't think so."

Clare watched her as she finished the dishes. Abigail knew there was more coming, so she turned slowly to face the questions that were going to be asked. Clare was finely tuned into Abigail's moods.

"You had a premonition about him, didn't you? Or about her?" Clare asked, wiping her hands on her apron. " Why do you let them touch you?"

"Sometimes people just touch people. Like old ladies. They reach out and touch people."

"You get all wigged out when you have a premonition. I know that's what happened."

"I don't get all wigged out."

"Like hell you don't. For having a gift like that your whole life, I'm surprised you don't handle it differently. You saw something."

Abigail wanted to argue with her cousin, but she knew there was no use. She'd been able to see the future or predict things her whole life. She'd always known when there was going to be a test in school, even before the teacher told them about it. There were a few times she found lost pets. She had told her mother to take a different route to the store the day that the semi carrying cars ended up rolling through the intersection and going through the front of the post office. Luckily, her mother had taken her advice, or she would have been at that intersection at that very moment.

It had been a game really, but the older she'd become, the more serious the premonitions became.

Her grandmother had a tumor, and she'd told her to have the doctors look for it. The visions and dreams had been very specific. When she held hands with her grandmother, Abigail would become ill, and pain would surge through her where she told her grandmother she thought they should check. Of course, her grandmother thought nothing of it, then died from the tumor Abigail had known was there. When Katie Meadows, the fifth-grade sister of a boy she'd grown up with, vanished in the night, Abigail told the police she thought they should look in the river, downstream. It was there they'd found her, caught on a branch in the frozen water.

That was when it was no longer a game. The police came after her, but there was no evidence that she'd done anything, or knew anything. The people in town thought she was a freak or sought her out for their own good. She couldn't freely go anywhere without people moving away from her, or searching her out. From then on she kept her thoughts to herself, but they'd always been spot on.

Things would come in dreams, and sometimes, they were just dreams. But when someone touched her, she would sometimes see things so vividly, as she had with the woman that day. She'd been told once, by a psychic her mother had taken her to, that if the person who touched her were open-minded, Abigail would see everything. Someone who was closed off to the world wouldn't let her see.

From then on, she'd tried never to touch too many people.

Close friends and family knew that if Abigail warned you about something, you took heed, especially after their grand-mother's death.

She knew when relationships weren't going to work out or even when a customer was going to walk in the door and cause her day to go badly. It wasn't ideal, but she could handle it.

The reason she'd moved to Golden and opened The Tea Shop with her cousin was to get out of the small town she'd grown up in. Her gift had become a nuisance, and there were a few times she feared for her own safety.

Since she'd moved, she hadn't had as many premonitions. That in itself was a gift as far as she was concerned. But once in a while, they still happened, just as they had today.

She didn't want to know that the woman she'd served today was going to become ill after her birthday. Her time was limited. She would succumb to Alzheimer's, and she was already becoming forgetful. It broke her heart into a million pieces because she'd found she very much enjoyed the woman. Perhaps the blessing would be if the woman never came back into the store, and neither did the man. But then that was a problem too. He was part of that premonition.

"So did you get some vibe on the old woman?" Clare asked as she turned to seal the container she'd made the egg salad in.

"Yeah. She's going to become very ill this next year. She probably won't make it through the spring."

"That sucks," Clare let out a defeated breath. "I'd be wigging out too if I knew that was going to happen to someone. Even if they're old."

Abigail nodded as she set the teapot on the shelf. "There was already some sadness that loomed between them. They had a history."

"Grandmother. Grandson."

"Maybe. I guess I'll find out." Abigail sat on the stool that Clare used by the prep table.

"Why do you say that?"

Abigail felt her face flush with heat and her heart began to beat a rapid rhythm in her chest. She wiped her damp palms on her apron before she looked up to see Clare's concerned face.

"Because that was the man I'm going to marry."

CHAPTER 3

*C*lare's mouth had dropped open, and her eyes were wide. This was not an unfamiliar sight to Abigail. Often when she offered up her premonitions, this was the kind of reaction she would get. And with the one she'd let spill out of her mouth, it was expected.

"Are you kidding me?" Clare dusted her hands on her apron and then rested them on the prep table. "You know that? You know that is the man you'll marry? What fun is that? Why him? Who is he?"

Abigail shrugged. "I don't know him. Well, I know his name. It was on the credit card slip. Carson Stone."

The corner of Clare's mouth turned up in a smile. "Abigail Stone. It has a nice ring to it."

Abigail cleared her throat and repeated the name of the man. "Carson Stone. Does it not ring any bells?"

A line formed between Clare's brows as she gave it serious thought. "Carson Stone. Carson Stone," she repeated. When her brows rose, Abigail knew she'd come to the conclusion on her own. "The business investor? Real estate guy?"

"Yep."

"The one who wants to tear down that church on Ford and one of the old college buildings for a strip mall?"

Abigail nodded.

"I thought he looked like a nice man," Clare went back to her work, obviously no longer impressed by Abigail's pending nuptials.

"We went to the city council meeting about the church."

"You, me, and five others. This town is much too big for only seven of us to fight for something, Abi. He's going to win."

Abigail ran her hand over the smooth surface of the table. "Maybe I can use this knowledge for good. Obviously, we're going to see each other again. I could work the situation."

"If you had a premonition, then that's fate, right? You can't change the course of things that are just going to happen —can you?"

"I guess we'll find out," she said as the chime above the door signaled, and she hopped off the stool.

CARSON WALKED TO THE COUNTER, HIS WALLET IN HIS HAND. THE waitress who had served them walked around the corner, but he noticed how the smile slipped away when she saw him. Hadn't he tipped her nicely?

"Hi—Abigail, right?"

"Yes," she said quickly, and the smile returned, but he wasn't so sure it was genuine.

"I think I left my credit card here."

Abigail searched through a stack of receipt books and shook her head. "No. It's not here. I'd check in your car, to the right of your seat. It fell between your seat and the console." As soon as she said it her eyes went wide. "I assume," her voice wavered. "That's where mine fall."

Carson chuckled. "I'll go look." Abigail turned as if to go back to the kitchen. "Can I ask you a question?" he began and watched as she turned back to him. Those blue eyes had ice to them, and he wondered what he might have done when he was there with Mrs. Winters that had her staring darts through him. "Do you take reservations?"

"Of course."

"Mrs. Winters would like to come for her birthday next month, and I told her I would see to that. She rather enjoyed your shop, and you," he added without stretching the truth.

Abigail's shoulders dropped, and the smile became more genuine. "She's a delightful woman."

"She is," he agreed as he leaned a hip up against the counter. "She has a lot of spunk, and life, and light."

He watched as she bit down on her bottom lip while she turned the page in the datebook on the counter. "She's well? Her health, I mean?"

It was an odd question, he thought, from someone who had just met the woman. "Very. I wouldn't challenge her to a fight. I think she'd win."

The muffled laugh that came from the woman who stood before him floated right to his chest.

"Her birthday is the 14th?"

Carson waited until Abigail lifted her eyes to meet his. "She told you that?"

"She must have."

"I don't remember her doing that. How did you know that was her birthday?"

For a moment she stared blankly at him, then blinked. "It's my birthday. I suppose I…"

Carson stood up straight. "Seriously? It's your birthday on the 14th of October?"

"Yes."

"I think that's a mighty interesting coincidence. She will love to hear that."

"Shall I put you down for tea? For two?"

"Three if you'll join us. A birthday celebration."

He watched as her face grew pale. "Oh, I don't…"

"It's okay. That was a bit forward of me. Besides, it's your birthday. You probably have big plans—like taking the day off."

"I'll be here."

"If it works out, I know she'd love it if you joined us. Even for one cup of tea," he quickly added before she could reject him again. "Two o'clock, does that work?"

"Huh?" Abigail dropped the pencil, grabbed for it, and nodded. "Yes. Two o'clock. I'll have it set up for her. Does she like a particular flower?"

"She's a sucker for roses. She can't get enough of them."

"Garden of them at the bottom of her porch?"

He felt the perma-grin on his face slip away. "She's lived here her whole life. Perhaps you've met her before. You seem to be very in tune with her."

"No. I'm new to the area myself. She just seems like the kind of woman who would have a beautiful garden of roses. I'll have some on the table for her."

"She'll enjoy that." Carson stepped back, slid his wallet into his pocket. "Thank you, Abigail. I look forward to seeing you next month."

He turned to leave but managed a look back at the woman, who looked positively horrified that he'd come back into the store. Why would that be, he wondered as he headed out to his car. What could he have possibly done or said in that short amount of time?

It should be something he was used to. People had an opinion about him, mostly because of his business. But really, he was progress in a town that needed some. Who needed an empty church that was rotting up from the foundation? Someone, someday was going to get hurt in a building like that. But sure as hell, the saviors of old things made him out to be the bad guy.

Carson climbed into his car and shut the door. On a whim,

though he'd already checked, he tucked his hand down between the seat and the center console and wiggled his fingers around. Then he felt it, the hard plastic of his credit card, and he moved a little more. A moment later he had it in his hand, and he laughed to himself.

He thought back to Abigail telling him where to look for the card, then the birthday coincidence, and the mention of the rose bushes. Honestly, if Mrs. Winters had passed twenty-some years earlier, he'd have thought she'd been reborn in Abigail. But as they were together just that afternoon, that now seemed a silly thought.

As he started the car and pulled away from the curb, he glanced back at the quaint store. Perhaps he'd give it a few days, and then he'd take his mother in for tea. She'd be elated, and he could check back in on Abigail.

CHAPTER 4

$\mathcal{A}$ new shipment of assorted candles had arrived when the friendly UPS man arrived. Pumpkin spice filled the air as October rolled in with its briskness.

The leaves on the aspen trees on the hill had begun their transformation, and Abigail couldn't wait for her free weekend to see the leaves changing. If she didn't hurry, all of the colors would be gone, and she'd be mesmerized by the snow instead.

She sniffed at the candle in her hand when a woman walked through the door letting in the breeze that was accompanying the October cool down.

Abigail set the candle down. "Welcome to The Tea Shop. Are you dining with us today, or browsing?"

The woman adjusted her purse on her shoulder. "I came a few minutes early. I'm meeting my son here for high tea, but I wanted to look at the gifts you had. I've looked in the window a few times, but haven't made it in myself yet."

"Wonderful. Will there be two of you for tea? I'll set you a table while you look around."

The woman smiled a familiar smile, yet Abigail knew she'd

never met the woman. "That would be delightful. He should be along shortly."

Abigail went to the kitchen and began to gather the china and tea set she'd be using for the woman and her son.

"We didn't have another tea on the books," Clare called from the cooler where she was taking inventory. "What are you setting up?"

"A walk-in. I'm glad too. It's been a bit too quiet around here. I know in December I'll be wishing for the break, but I'd rather have the business than a quiet afternoon."

Abigail took the silver, plates, and napkins to the table near the window. She preferred to sit customers there so other possible customers would see them having a good time. Their lunch rush had been quiet too, but that was expected on a Tuesday.

When she was finished, she made her way back to the counter and noticed the woman had an arm full of the new candles, and one of the handmade aprons draped over her arm.

"Can I take a few of those for you?" Abigail moved to her. "It looks as if you found a few things."

"I hadn't thought of Christmas shopping here. But I think that's exactly what I'm doing," she laughed as she unloaded her finds into Abigail's hands. "Did you make the apron?"

A warmth filled her cheeks as she smiled. "My mother makes them and sends them to me to sell."

"They are adorable. I haven't seen hand stitched items like these in years. Is she sending more? I'd like two more, just like that one."

A flutter lit in Abigail's chest. "If you're interested, I can put in a special order to her. It would take about two weeks for them to arrive."

"I would love that. I'll pay for them today if that's okay. That'll make it much easier for me."

"Certainly. I'll get this wrapped up for you, and you can check out whenever you're ready."

"Okay, I want to look at your pastries first. My mother would adore a sweet this afternoon. She's in an assisted living facility. I sneak her in something special every once in a while," she said with a wide grin, and Abigail's thoughts went right to her grandmother. They had done that for her as well.

When the woman had finished her shopping, she walked back to the counter where Abigail had wrapped and bagged her new treasures. She had printed out a receipt and showed the woman each item.

"You are very precise and organized, aren't you?" The woman smiled as she handed Abigail her credit card.

"I want to help make your experience as pleasant as possible," Abigail said as she scanned the card and the door opened again.

When she looked up, the eye contact she made with Carson Stone nearly had her knees giving out. She hadn't expected to see him until his reservation in another two weeks. Oh, she certainly hoped he hadn't come to cancel them because her premonition came true.

It was then that the woman turned to him and wrapped her arms around him. "I came to do a little shopping before you arrived," she said as she brushed her hand down the lapel of his suit coat.

Abigail looked down at the credit card in her hand. Patricia Stone. This was his mother.

She gripped the counter and tried to suck in a breath, but not before Carson moved around to her and put his arm around her waist.

"Why don't you sit down. You went white as a sheet," he said moving her toward the stool where she felt her knees finally buckle.

"What's going on?" Clare hurried out of the kitchen and moving past Carson. "Are you okay? Abi, you're pale."

Abigail cleared her throat. "I'm fine. Everyone stop fussing over me," she said as she pushed away the fog that had clouded her brain and stood, realizing Carson's arm was still around her, though she saw nothing in that fog that told her of their pending future together.

"I assume you set that pretty table for my mother and I," he said softly in her ear. "You're going to sit with us for a moment until you're feeling just right."

The argument pierced her tongue, but somehow it refused to surface as he helped her across the store to the little table she'd set only a few minutes earlier.

Carson sat her in one of the chairs, his mother sat in the other, and he pulled another from a table for himself.

The look of worry in Patricia Stone's eyes had her wondering if she'd said anything at that moment when her world began to spin. Had she blurted out the words that she was going to marry her son? Wouldn't he have laughed or argued?

When her mind cleared, she let out a long breath. Carson held up one of the glasses of ice water to her.

"Sip this."

"I'm fine really," she argued again.

"Sip."

To appease him, she sipped the water, noticing that Clare stood in the doorway to the kitchen watching the entire ordeal. What kind of help was she anyway?

"I'm fine now."

Carson reached a hand to her cheek, and still, nothing moved through her as it had when Mrs. Winters touched her, or when she realized that it had been his mother who wore the familiar smile—his smile.

"I think you just might be okay." He sat back in his seat, blocking her in with his knee. "I know you work in a restaurant, but did you eat today?"

"Of course—I—well, I think I..." she stopped when she realized that in fact, she hadn't eaten at all. She'd woken late, run out of her apartment and to the store, and they'd had a pastry rush earlier that morning. Clare usually made sure they had something to eat for lunch, but they'd worked to make sure there were pastries for the after-work crowd too. Then the UPS man had delivered the candles on what was to be a quiet afternoon. "I guess I didn't eat after all."

Carson lifted his eyes to Clare and gave a nod. "She's making you a little something. You can sit here with us."

The panic returned. "No. You're here to have tea with your mother. I promise you I'm fine. No need to fuss over me," she explained as she wiped her hands on her apron. But she hadn't stood quickly enough. Clare approached the table with a sandwich on a petite plate. If it weren't rude, she would have scowled. Instead, she graciously accepted the plate.

"I'll get your teas started," Clare offered. "Which ones might I offer you?"

"I'd love the spiced tea I saw on display," Patricia said sweetly. "Carson will have Earl Grey."

Clare disappeared into the kitchen, and Abigail went on to eat her sandwich. The sooner she finished, the quicker she could get back to work. She found herself begging any spirit that could hear her to bring in more customers. But they must have been ignoring her. No one even walked in front of the store.

"So, Abigail, when did you open this cute little shop?" Patricia asked.

"We've only been open less than a year. This has been a perfect location though."

"It's so quaint." She lifted her eyes to Carson. "You brought Mrs. Winters here?"

He nodded, easing back in his chair and crossing his leg over the other. "I did. I'm bringing her back for her birthday, which happens to be Abigail's birthday too."

Abigail chewed slower, afraid that she just might choke on the sandwich.

"You don't say," Patricia pressed her hands together as if she might applaud. "You and Ellie Winters share a birthday. What a special day. She's taken with my Carson."

Abigail took the napkin from the table and wiped her mouth. "I thought maybe she was your grandmother."

Carson shook his head and that same smile that graced his mother's lips formed on his. "She's the grandmother of a dear friend. He passed years ago, and his grandmother and I remained close."

Abigail could almost hear Clare swooning in the kitchen. Okay, so he wasn't the dark and sinister man they'd decided he was, but she supposed he still intended to tear down the church on Ford.

Why had her premonition come when Mrs. Winters had touched her, but not when Carson had? And when she realized the woman was his mother, why had her knees gone weak and her brain turned to mush.

Was it a fluke?

The only way to know for sure was to touch him again.

Forcing a smile to her lips, she stood, and so did he. "I'm feeling fine now. Let me get the rest of your tea service. Will you be having sandwiches and scones? Or would you like the dessert platter?"

Carson exchanged a glance with his mother. "I'd like that one you brought for me and Mrs. Winters. With the few desserts. And I'll tell you now, I'll need some of that lemon cake to go for my father."

Patricia did applaud now. "Oh, he will love that, Carson."

When his eyes shifted back to Abigail, the thought of rising on her toes and kissing the handsome man in front of her crossed her mind. That would certainly tell her if he were the man she would marry. Of course, that might make him stalk out of the store because she was crazy. Instead, she eased a hand on his arm as if to pass.

Nothing.

No spark. No vision. Not even a hitch in her breath.

It had to be a fluke. If this were the man she was destined to marry, she'd have felt something. As it was, he was an investor in her town, who had his sights on tearing down one of the most beautiful buildings around. Well, she still planned on putting a stop to that.

CHAPTER 5

There were no more dizzy spells or insights into the man who now dined with his mother.

Abigail watched from the kitchen with Clare right behind her.

"You didn't feel anything?" Clare asked for the third time.

"No. Nothing. I don't think my premonition was correct. I might be slipping some since I've come here." And she thanked God for that. It wasn't a gift she truly wanted. "Maybe I was seeing something else when I touched Mrs. Winters' hand."

"Maybe she's the one who is going to marry him."

That caused Abigail to chuckle, and she moved away from the door. "Now that would be a story wouldn't it?" She sat on the stool at the prep table as Clare worked on the pastries for the next morning. "He said Mrs. Winters was the grandmother of a friend who died. What kind of man keeps a relationship with a friend's grandmother?"

"Doesn't seem like the tyrant we've made him out to be would do such a thing."

Abigail fidgeted with the hem on her apron. "No, but he still is going to tear down that church."

"I say you make a move on him, see him for a bit, then when

he's head over heels in love with you, tell him not to hurt the church."

"Your mind is in the clouds," she joked, but honestly she'd thought of that herself. "When the church is safe, I break his heart?"

"Why not? He's just a man."

Just a man, she thought about it. Just a man who had taken a phone call in the middle of having tea with his mother. He'd just excused himself outside. What kind of man did that kind of thing?

Abigail hopped down from the stool and made her way to the table where Patricia Stone spread clotted cream on her scone.

"How is everything?" Abigail asked as Patricia looked up at her.

"Oh, darling, this is the most lovely place I've ever seen. Before I leave, you remind me to make a reservation to bring my mother here, and then I want to reserve a few tables for my book club. They are going to eat this place up," she said on air filled with delight. "He's going to be a moment, and you're not busy. Sit, will you?"

"I don't—I shouldn't—okay, just for a moment."

Abigail sat down in the seat Carson had vacated.

When the bell above the front door jingled, Abigail looked up and saw Carson walk in from outside. He looked at her and his mother sitting together at the table and quickly pulled up another chair.

Abigail started to rise, but his hand quickly came to her arm to stop her. "There's no need to go anywhere. You're welcome to join us for a few more minutes," he said.

Abigail looked down to where his hand touched her skin, and there was no spark. How had she seen the premonition she had. It was so vivid. She thought back to the moment when Mrs. Winters had touched her. She had clearly seen them, and they were getting married. Perhaps she was wrong. It had never happened before, but anything was possible. However, as his fingers lingered on her skin it forced her to look up into those eyes. Those dark brown eyes. Abigail felt her breath hitch, and she had to force herself to breathe in. There was no longer a reason to believe that this was the man she was going to marry. After all, if she were to peg the man she was supposed to marry, as the premonition had shown her, there should have been some kind of spark. But then again, wasn't she angry with him? It was almost as if she couldn't remember why she was angry, but then she remembered. He was going to tear down that church on Ford Street, and she wasn't going to have any part of that. In fact, it became much clearer now as she looked into the dark brown eyes of chocolate, that this was supposed to be something she used to her benefit. She was going to stop him.

Abigail gave him a sweet smile. "I might join you for just a few more moments," she said softly. As she sat back in her seat, his hand released her arm as he grabbed a scone and slathered it with the clotted cream, just as his mother had. She noticed their hands, and how distinctly the same they were. Though his were much more rugged, there was no mistaking that they were related, even from their hands. Without looking as if she were trying too hard, Abigail looked at his mother and studied the structure of her face. Perhaps he looked like his father, she thought.

"While the two of you finish up your tea, why don't I go box of some of that lemon cake," she offered, noticing that Clare was standing in the kitchen watching them.

Carson looked over his shoulder towards the kitchen. "It seems you don't have any other customers right now, why doesn't she join us too?" he said.

The horror in that very sentence struck her. Abigail was absolutely sure she did not want Clare to come talk to him. Wasn't she as mad as Abigail was about the church on Ford Street? Of course she was. But then again, it was Clare who had decided he wasn't the tyrant they'd thought he was.

"We have a large group coming in tomorrow. A sewing guild," she said. "It will be the first Wednesday of the month, and that means they will be here to have early tea. She's busy making all their scones."

Patricia had moved in closer to the table, and her hands had come together almost as if in prayer. "A sewing guild? That sounds absolutely delightful. Where do they meet to sew?"

Abigail looked at her with a blank stare. "To tell you the truth, I never thought to ask. I guess I should do that. That would be good customer service."

Carson chuckled, and that had her turning to look at him.

"You have good customer service," he said admiringly. "Do you sew yourself?"

She shook her head. "No. I haven't sewn since I was in Girl Scouts." Then she thought about that experience. It hadn't gone very well. Juliet Harper, the leader's daughter, had touched her in a game of Hey Rover, and it was then that she knew immediately that this girl had been the one stealing everybody's lunch money. When she told the teacher the next day, everyone assumed that Abigail was a snitch, and perhaps the one that was stealing it to begin with. Abigail was able to acknowledge a universal gift. Because after that day, she spent the rest of her recesses in the library, reading books. She found a lot more fun in that.

Carson picked up his teacup, and held it towards his lips. "My mother loves to quilt." He smiled widely. "Perhaps you could find out who their leader is."

Patricia put a hand over her son's. "He would do anything to get me out of his office."

Whatever the inside joke was, it had Carson laughing. "It's time you retire," he argued. "She just doesn't seem to like the word."

"Oh, I like the word just fine. I just think you need me in your office."

Abigail looked at Carson. "What do you do for a living?"

The smile curled up the side of his mouth, and he looked at his mother. "Would you like to tell her?"

"I'm so proud of him, I like to brag," she said with her own matching smile. "Carson is a real estate developer. He buys buildings and invests in businesses. It's wonderful for the economy, but not everyone thinks that's a good thing."

Abigail pushed her shoulders back. "Why is that a bad thing?"

Carson took a bite of his scone. "Not everyone likes innovation. Many people want decrepit buildings to stand when they are hazardous, and hard to heat and fix." He waved his hand in the air as if to erase the conversation. "It's what I do, and she likes to babysit me."

His eyes met Abigail's as he said it, and it was then she felt that spark.

She pushed herself back from the table and stood. "I'll be back with that lemon cake," she said hurriedly as she went to the kitchen as quickly as possible.

As expected, Clare was waiting just around the wall. "What did they say to you? You sat down with them. You never sit down with customers. You don't even sit down with the sewing guild."

"Keep your voice down," she scolded. "I felt a spark," she whispered.

Abigail moved around the prep table, and over to where the new loaves of lemon bread cooled on a rack. She took down a cardboard box with its cellophane top and laid a decorative paper doily in the bottom of the box. Carefully, she took the nicest loaf of lemon bread, which Clare had recently iced, and placed it in the box.

When she turned back from the counter, Clare was standing right in front of her. "You're not gonna say anything more about the spark?"

Abigail thought she hadn't meant to say that much about the spark. "He has nice eyes. But that's all I'm going to say. It wasn't like the premonition. He's not who I think he is. He still the man who's going to destroy this town by tearing down all the buildings."

"Did he tell you that?"

She thought for a moment. "No, he didn't tell me that. But his mother did say that he wants to renovate the area and invest in the businesses."

"Perhaps he'd like to invest in ours and pay the gas bill," Clare joked.

Abigail moved around her cousin toward the station where they kept tissue paper and ribbons. "I'd rather leave this alone," she said as she pulled a long, red ribbon from the spindle and cut it with a pair of scissors. "To tell you the truth, this is all very silly. I haven't had a premonition since I moved here. Well, not one of any significance. Not until I met Mrs. Winters that is. I'm guessing I've gotten my wires crossed," she said as she tied a ribbon around the box. "I do think he's a nice enough man. I don't think he's my future husband. And I'd really like to think that maybe Mrs. Winters won't get sick." That one didn't feel right in her heart. That premonition seemed to be as real as any she'd ever had. "I'm going to take this out to them for his father. His mother seems to think he will like the lemon cake just as much as Mrs. Winters did."

Clare crossed her arms in front of her and cocked her head to the side. "If he weren't a tyrant who tore down old buildings, you'd be head over heels in love with him already, wouldn't you?"

Abigail wasn't even going to consider an answer to that, let alone give it any thought. Because unfortunately, she was sure her cousin was correct.

CHAPTER 6

*W*hen Carson's mother had called that night, to tell him that his father loved the lemon cake, his mind went directly to Abigail.

He'd spent some time on the internet when he couldn't work because she was on his mind. The website for her tea store was as quaint as the store itself.

Abigail Weston, he'd learned from the bio, the name rang in his ears like a song, he thought. She didn't seem to like him much. That much he caught. But the big question was why? He hadn't said anything horrible to her. He hadn't tried to tear down her building. In fact, he hadn't even heard of her little business until Mrs. Winters had wanted to go there. Why was it he hadn't heard of her little business, he wondered as he set up his coffee pot for the next morning's brewing. Carson always knew when new restaurants or gift shops were opening in his town. Golden wasn't small. But he had his hand in everything.

Carson set the coffee pot to brew tomorrow morning at 5 AM, that was usually when he returned home from the gym. Of course, now, he wondered if Abigail had coffee or tea in the mornings when she woke up. He let out a long breath. Why was he even bothering?

Oh, she was cordial enough. And he knew that his mother and Mrs. Winters were well-liked by Abigail, that much he could tell. But there was something about the way she looked at him. It didn't give him a good vibe.

Carson Stone wasn't somebody who didn't get what he wanted. No, he thought as he walked to the bedroom, since his living room was currently under construction, and turned on his TV. Carson Stone always got what he wanted, and right now he wanted to know more about Abigail Weston. The woman intrigued him. Her business sense intrigued him—even her choice in footwear.

He smiled to himself as he turned on the news. Sometimes getting to know people became a game. It was how he got to be invested in their businesses, their city, and eventually buy their land. Well, when he thought of it that way, it did make him sound like a horrible man, and that wasn't who he was.

Carson enjoyed seeing new things grow. Just like he enjoyed Mrs. Winters' rose garden. Tearing down the old, and building it with new. It was an adventure. How come everybody didn't see it that way?

Thinking about that, only made him realize that next week he'd have another one of those community meetings where everybody came to yell at him. Sure, like his mother said, perhaps if that many people were against you, you should rethink your actions. But honestly, the buildings were falling down. When the homeless moved into them, it would be dreadful. And not because they were homeless, but because somebody was going to get hurt. After all, how many old buildings had he and his brother gone through when they were younger? Maybe it was that one day in that decrepit old mansion that people thought was haunted, when he fell through the floor, that made him want to take down old buildings. He would never forget, he sat there with his leg dangling down from the second floor into the dining room because the floor had given out when he jumped from one beam to another. Had the other beam given out, he might have died. He and his brother kept that secret. Oh, wouldn't their mother have been angry? If she were a violent woman, he thought, she might've spanked them until they couldn't have sat down. But as it was, Patricia Stone never lifted a finger against her children.

His mother might not always agree with his career preference, but she supported him one hundred percent, and so did his father. It wasn't so much that they didn't agree with the career itself, but like many others, didn't agree with the methods.

There was no way around it he thought as he pressed the button on the remote control. If he didn't argue to take down the old buildings, they would still be up. No progress would be made in the city. No new businesses would come to the area. And again, another old building would be left there to rot, and somebody would get hurt.

But in the middle of a community meeting, perhaps he lost his temper a few too many times. He tried not to, but it was hard. People were there to attack him, attack his character. Often they came out yelling first, so it wasn't his fault.

Carson closed his eyes for a minute and listened to the infomercial that played on the TV. Then, as if something had zipped into his brain, he sat straight up.

The day he had met Abigail in her store when he had taken Mrs. Winters for tea, he had thought, only briefly, that he had seen Abigail somewhere before. As he had been sitting there wallowing in what was to come with that community meeting, he realized that was where he had seen Abigail Weston. Yes, she had been there when they announced plans to tear down the church on Ford Street and build a new outdoor shopping center.

Now that he thought about it, her cousin Clare had been with her. He hadn't remembered Abigail speaking, but Clare had. They hadn't caused a scene or anything. Perhaps they didn't get a chance. There were others who had a greater opinion on his new project.

Well, it did explain a lot. No wonder she looked at him with such distaste. She, like everyone else, thought he was the bad guy.

What would it take to make her change her mind?

One thing about Carson Stone, he was charming when he wanted to be. Hadn't Mrs. Winters told him that at least a million times?

Carson turned off the TV. Tomorrow, he thought, he would go to The Tea Shop while that sewing group was there. He would get more information, for his mother, he would tell them. But in all honesty, he wanted just a few more minutes to be around Abigail.

He smiled to himself as he pulled off his shirt and threw it into the hamper. He did enjoy a good challenge.

CHAPTER 7

*C*arson could hear laughter as he approached The Tea Shop on that brisk Thursday morning. He'd worked it up in his head what he was going to say when he went inside. Of course, he couldn't wait to see Abigail's face when he walked through the door.

He assumed there would be some groaning, but it would be inaudible.

Her eyes would grow wide before she pressed a smile to those rosy lips. When he visited with Mrs. Winters, he'd been charming, as he always was when he was around Mrs. Winters. When he visited with his mother, he was polite and very interested. Now he would be there with an entire store full of women whom he supposed he could win over with his charm. Sure, some of them might know who he is and have the same opinion of him as Abigail did, but in the end he'd win them over, too.

Carson passed by the front window and looked inside to see that every table was occupied. Each woman had one of those fancy Prussian cups in front of her, and a plate of breakfast pastries. They were talking, sharing small needlecraft, and laughing. He could hear the laughter from where he stood outside the door. It was time to make his entrance. "Move over Prince Charming, here comes Carson Stone," he humored out loud to himself.

As far as Abigail was concerned, Clare had outdone herself for this morning's tea. There were scones, chocolate pastries, fruit pastries, fruit trays, and a chocolate mousse because Clare simply thought it was appropriate to have more dessert with such a sweet breakfast. Perhaps next month, Abigail thought, they could bring in an omelet station. Maybe she could work something out with the hotel down the street. Cross marketing was important in such a small area.

She had just gathered up a set of dishes and was bringing out another for Mrs. Duncan who adored her chocolate croissants, when the door to the shop opened, and the bell above it chimed.

As she moved from the kitchen to the table, she looked up to see Carson Stone walk through the door. Managing to keep the smile on her face, she greeted him. "I didn't expect to see you this morning. What can I get for you? Something to go I presume."

She watched him scan the room and each woman look up at him. He flashed that smile, oh that smile that had burned into her brain. It had the effect it was supposed to have on all the women in the room. A few of them said hello to him by name. Others asked who he might be.

Abigail dropped off the plates, asked if there was anything else she could do for Mrs. Duncan, and then made her way back to the front of the store.

She stepped around the counter and pulled out the biggest box she had. "Are you taking pastries to your office?" If he was going to keep coming into her store to bother her, she might as well make some money off of it.

Carson had taken a breath as if he were going to argue with her, but then he flashed that smile again. "I came in for a cup of coffee and to talk to your ladies. But you fix me up a box, and I'll take them into the office. Send me with some of your business cards too. I'll bet you'll have a busy lunch."

Abigail gritted her teeth. "I'll make sure you have the perfect assortment. Why were you coming to talk to the ladies?" she asked quietly.

Carson leaned in over the counter. "I was serious when I said I thought my mother should retire. I think it would be a good thing to have her in one of the sewing guilds. She would enjoy it immensely. Who might I talk to about that?"

Abigail looked up and scanned the room. Mrs. Duncan was enjoying her second chocolate pastry, so perhaps she might be pleasant to him. Abigail pointed at the woman who nearly over-flowed the tiny chair that was positioned at the end of one of the tables.

"Mrs. Duncan has been the guild's president for a decade. She's very picky. Are you sure you would like your mother to be part of that?"

"My mother is very picky too," he said as he turned around. "I think she should fit in just fine."

Abigail watched him walk away and make a path straight for Mrs. Duncan. Mrs. Duncan looked up at him with narrowed eyebrows. Carson stuck out his hand, said something, and a moment later Mrs. Duncan was laughing that jolly laugh that took over the store. Abigail began to fill the box of pastries. She supposed she shouldn't be surprised that even Mrs. Duncan had fallen victim to Carson's charm. After all, she knew what he was all about, and she fell for his charm too.

By the time Carson had returned to the front counter, Abigail had the large box full of pastries ready to go. She gave him his total and watched as he pulled his wallet from his pocket without even a thought. Though she was happy for the sale, she kinda hoped he might be put off by it.

"Will your mother be at work this morning?" She asked him, while she ran his credit card.

"I'm expecting her."

"I slipped in one of those chocolate pastries that Mrs. Duncan seems to favor. Before she eats them all." Carson laughed at that. "Tell her I look forward to her book club next month."

"So she called yesterday after we left, huh? I thought she might. She didn't mention it though."

"Does she run everything by you," Abigail asks snidely as she handed him back his credit card and slip to sign.

Carson scribbled an illegible line of squiggles on to the receipt and handed it back to her. In the exchange, their fingers touched, and for the first time, Abigail saw something that hadn't been there before.

"It was nice to see you this morning, Abigail. Enjoy the rest of your day."

She bit down on her lip hard enough she could taste a hint of blood. As Carson picked up the box and turned around to leave the store she called out to him to stop him.

Quickly moving around the counter, she hurried to the door and opened it. "Your hands are full. Let me help you to your car."

Carson studied her for a moment, perhaps considering whether she had lost her mind or not. "Perfectly able to carry this box. No need for any help. Thank you anyway."

She reached for his arm but his jacket covered his skin, and his bare hands held the box. Perhaps if she touched him once more, she'd know if what she saw was real.

He scanned another look over her. "Did I forget something?"

What was she supposed to say? She'd been so rude to him, and now she was holding on to him. "We over estimated for the party. Clare is great at planning. But I thought if you came by after work, you could pick up what we have left, pastries that is, and take them to the office tomorrow."

With a slow and thoughtful nod he said, "Come tonight for pastries for tomorrow?"

Oh, that did sound dumb. Abigail smiled sweetly and gave his arm a gentle squeeze since she was still holding on to him. "It would be nice to see you again today. If you don't want the pastries…"

"I'll come back by," he agreed. "What time do you close?"

"Six."

"I'll be here before then," he offered as she released him. "I'll see you later."

Abigail watched him climb into his black Audi and drive away with a wave.

When she turned back to the store, she noticed an entire room of ladies with their noses nearly pressed against the window. So, she might have just saved the man's life, but now she was going to have to fight off all the gossip. Seriously, she was too nice to have this curse. Why couldn't it just go away?

CHAPTER 8

*T*he staff in Carson's office was more than happy to have the enormous box of pastries he purchased for them. And of course, his mother was equally as pleased with her special pastry and the phone number for Mrs. Duncan.

"I'm going to give her a call right now," his mother said as she dashed by him with chocolate on her fingers. He laughed and picked up the phone that rang on his desk.

He knew his mind wasn't much into his work, when Emily, his assistant, came back in for the third time to have a contract signed.

"Are you sure you're feeling okay? You never miss these things," she scolded. Though it was hard to take a scolding from a twenty-five-year-old, he thought, he understood her concern.

"I'm fine. I just have a lot on my mind. Thank you for checking these over."

"Thank you for the pastries this morning. I haven't had one of their pastries since they opened. I may have to start going over there and getting my coffee and my breakfast."

Carson smiled at that. He had told Abigail he'd bring her business. Maybe she'd find out he was serious about it.

As Emily left his office, he thought about Abigail. Most of the time she was trying to rush him out of her store. What was with her grabbing on to him this morning? It was as if she didn't want him to leave for work. That was a very strange feeling. But with his mind not being able to focus, he thought he'd leave a little bit early and head over to the tea store. What would it hurt if he had to hang around for a while?

Throughout the day, Emily delivered messages to him regarding the community meeting that was to be had the following week. Investors wanted to know their money was safe. Contractors wanted to know if they'd still have contracts to count on. And then there were the hate messages. One person called him names he'd never heard of, perhaps that was Emily's rendition of the message as she read it—all the while her face grew redder. Someone threatened to kill his cat, which he didn't have, and he wondered why someone would choose to be so violent. A building wasn't in comparison to a life, which the next person threatened to take—his life, that was.

It was the voicemail he received around three that had him growing uneasy in his chair. "Churches are sacred. That fancy car of yours is sacred to you. I'm sure you'll rethink your plans when you see what happens to it."

Carson hit the button to turn off the speaker on his phone and glanced out the window of his office to where he could see his car parked in the lot across the street. The car was still there and looked exactly as it had that morning. However, the longer he sat in his office, the more uncomfortable he'd become. Perhaps a nice cup of tea would calm his nerves.

After informing Emily and his mother that he was leaving, on a business matter, he cautiously walked to his car flinching as he pressed the button to unlock the door. When nothing happened, he climbed inside and exercised equally as much caution when turning on the engine.

Okay, they'd gotten to him. He was a bit spooked. Perhaps

he'd watched too many horror flicks. It would all be forgotten by tomorrow, he decided, as he drove out of the lot and headed toward Abigail's store.

Carson parked his car across the street from the quaint little store. He sat there for a moment. Inside, he could see Abigail aligning the shelves with new collectibles. At the moment, she didn't seem to have any customers.

Why a tea shop? What made her decide that that was what she wanted to do with her life? It was quaint and cute, just as she was. It fit her, he thought, as he watched her do her work.

He looked at the building that housed the little tea shop. It had been renovated only a few years before he started getting involved in the real estate industry. What had it been, he tried to remember. His mother would know, he was sure of it. It had always been retail, and had always had some kind of cute store in it. He'd have to admit, if he had purchased the building, perhaps it wouldn't be so quaint.

He understood why people got upset with him. What he didn't understand was why they had to threaten him.

As Abigail disappeared from view, Carson stepped out of his car. He casually strolled across the street and opened the door to the tea shop. From the kitchen, he could hear someone humming a familiar tune, though he couldn't place it. Wait, was she singing Mandy by Barry Manilow? He chuckled to himself. Yes, she was as quaint and cute as her little shop.

THE MUSIC PLAYING ON THE RADIO ALWAYS MADE ABIGAIL THINK OF her mother. She had an affinity for the 70's, though Abigail never quite understood why. The shop was quiet this afternoon, and Clare had gone home early. There were no high teas on the book. She expected that no one would stop by on their way home. But she would stay open 'til six. She wasn't one to go against the little sign in the window.

Abigail collected the freshly pressed napkins that would go on the tables for tomorrow morning's book club brunch. She sauntered out of the kitchen and the flash of a man at the door caught her eye. Suddenly her singing got caught in her throat, and she nearly let out a scream.

"I didn't hear you come in. Why did you sneak in?" She scolded Carson.

"I certainly didn't sneak in. The bell above the door chimed. You were too busy belting out that song. Manilow?"

"My mother adores him."

"So does my mother. Perhaps we should get them together."

Abigail set the napkins on the table closest to her and brushed her hands over her apron.

"My mother lives in Kansas City. I don't think they'll be dining together anytime soon."

"You never know."

Abigail glanced down at her watch. "I didn't expect you so early. I can't box everything up yet. Just in case."

"It just so happens I have nothing to do. Maybe I'll just sit here and listen to you sing Copacabana."

She didn't like the humor that lit in his eyes when he teased her. However, perhaps having him there would be better. She hadn't liked what she saw when she touched him that morning. She didn't truly understand. She had the keen sense that somebody wanted to hurt him.

"I don't perform in public," she said picking up the napkins again. "I could, however, make you a tea plate. Earl Grey?"

Carson studied her for a moment. "If you were gonna sit down and have tea with me, what kind of tea would you have?"

Abigail gripped the napkins in her hand. She'd brought this on herself. She'd invited him back, and she'd done it by grabbing his arm and touching him. The man must think she was a lunatic. Well, there were times she thought she was a lunatic, herself.

Abigail gave it some thought. "With the seasons changing, I have found that I liked the spice tea best."

"You're not one of those pumpkin spice latte people are you?"

"No, I dislike the spiced lattes. But I won't lie, it does go well with pumpkin bread."

"Sit with me. Have some tea and pumpkin bread with me."

Abigail took a breath to argue, but then looking around the store, she realized it would be futile to do so.

"Fine, I'll sit with you. Put these napkins on each table. On the right-hand side of the plate. And don't mess them up," she ordered as she handed him the pile of napkins.

Carson took them. She avoided eye contact or touching him. Turning around, she headed back to the kitchen to find the pumpkin bread that Clare had made earlier that morning.

CHAPTER 9

*W*ith pumpkin bread and little dollops of butter on a Prussian plate, Abigail walked back out to the storefront carrying the silver tray set. Carson was seated at the table closest to the kitchen. She noticed he had taken off his tie and loosened the button on his collar.

Her eyes darted to the other tables where he had laid the napkins down just as he had been instructed to. The chuckle he let out directed her attention back to him.

"Did I do a good job, boss?"

"No need to be snarky. But yes, you did a fine job." She set the tray on the table and sat down across from him. She took each plate off the silver tray, and then the saucer and cup as well. He watched her every move, she noted. When all of the dishes were on the table, she stood again and picked up the tray. This time he grabbed her wrist.

"The tray can sit on the table. You're not serving me as a customer."

"Then what am I doing?"

"You are having some tea and pumpkin bread, with me, as friends."

49

Abigail stood there with his fingers touching her skin. But there was calm. No longer did she see a threat to his life. The breath that she knew she was holding, she finally let go.

"Friends? We don't really know each other."

"Well, then I guess we should get to know each other. Friends are just strangers who got to know each other, correct?"

His finger still lingered on her wrist. "Fine. I guess we're becoming friends." She set the tray back on the table and took her seat.

He was watching her again as she set up her teacup. She tried not to let it make her nervous, but she noticed her hand shook when she held the tea strainer over the cup.

"Are you going to make your tea?" she asked, noting that he had sat back, very comfortable.

"I'm having quite a nice time watching you make your tea."

Abigail swallowed the lump in her throat. She wasn't afraid of this man. If she were, she would have let that rock fly through his window as he drove away from his office. But somehow, he ended up there in her store earlier than anticipated.

She set the silver pot of water down on the table, clasped her hands in her lap, and looked up at the handsome stranger across from her. "Why do you keep coming by my store?"

Carson pursed his lips. "I like the view," he said.

"I didn't invite you back here this afternoon to flirt with you," she informed him. "I was being nice to a man who has brought me a lot of business in the last couple weeks. Your mother will be here tomorrow morning with her book club."

"She did mention that. I think you'll find her friends delightful."

"So you're just being friendly because we're in business in the same city?"

Carson leaned in, moving his teacup and his plate out of his way. He rested his forearms on the table and clasped his hands together.

"Abigail, I think you can read me just fine. Yes, I want your shop to succeed. I happen to have a lot of women in my life who enjoy your shop, too. But I'm going to guess that you're a smart woman. You need more hints for me to tell you that I'm attracted to you?"

Abigail twisted her apron in her hands under the table. "Can't say I expected you to say that."

"I'll be disappointed if you don't think I'm attractive too."

That made Abigail laugh, and she hadn't expected to laugh. She thought about the premonition she had the day that Mrs. Winters touched her. They looked happy. Was this the beginning of that fate? Was this the beginning of what would become? The premonition showed her that the two of them would be married. Was he a man she learned to love? Or was he the tyrant that she had made him out to be? At that very moment, she wasn't sure which one she wanted him to be.

She picked up her teacup and steadied it with both hands. Removing the strainer, she took a sip. It didn't seem to settle her nerves any.

Setting the cup back on the saucer, she clasped her hands again in her lap again. "I'm not used to this part of making friends."

"I came to that assumption on my own. Will you have dinner with me tomorrow night?"

Abigail sucked in a breath to speak, then nearly choked on it when no words came out. It forced her to cough, and she pressed her hand to her chest while he looked on.

"Dinner? We've been in each other's presence maybe five times. Does that constitute dinner?"

Carson sat back in his chair and folded his arms in front of him. His smile was enormous, and his cheeks pinked as if he held a secret behind those eyes.

"How long do you think somebody needs before they know they love somebody?"

"Love somebody?" Her voice jumped another octave. "Are you telling me you are in love with me?"

He laughed a hearty laugh and sat back up straight in his chair. This time he poured the water into his cup and set the strainer in the water.

"Mrs. Winters knew her husband for seventy-two hours before they got married. It was love at first sight."

"Perhaps things were different back then."

"Perhaps."

Abigail busied her hands by breaking her pumpkin bread into fourths. She took the petite knife and buttered one of the pieces. "You have a very special relationship with Mrs. Winters."

Carson nodded, the smile still wide on his lips. "I do. We helped each other through a very hard time. I suppose we still help each other out through that very hard time." The smile remained on his lips, but his eyes told another story.

Abigail sipped her tea. "Since we're friends. Can you tell me about that hard time?"

Carson broke his bread into pieces, much as she had, but he didn't add butter to the bite he took. He took another moment to collect himself. "Jeffery Winters and I were best friends from the time we were five years old. He was like a brother to me." The smile was back as he brushed his fingers through his hair. "Junior year, just shy of his seventeenth birthday, we headed up Lookout Mountain for a guys' night."

Abigail could feel the change in the story coming. Instinctively, she reached her hand across the table and placed it on his.

He looked up at her with sad eyes, and her heart broke into two.

"Every part of that night could've been avoided. Every single part." He looked down at their hands, hers covering his, and moved so that he intertwined their fingers together. "We had all intentions of spending the night there, back in the wooded area. We each had a six-pack of some nasty beer. And though we drove to the top, we had no plans to drive back down. We were smarter than that."

His thumb grazed over her knuckles. The intimacy lit a fire in her chest.

"We were as drunk as any seventeen-year-old boys could get on cheap beer. We had blankets on the hard ground, stars above our heads, and a little fire in a fire pit."

"If you didn't drive down the mountain, what happened?" She had to ask. It was as if he wasn't getting to the end fast enough for her heart to break again.

"Jeffery got up. It must've been two o'clock in the morning. All we can think is that he got up to go to the bathroom. Then there was the most horrific scream." He squeezed her fingers in his. "He fell off the side of the mountain. They couldn't save him. The fall, the rocks—his injuries were too severe."

Abigail raised her free hand to her lips, which now trembled. Tears welled in her eyes. "Carson, I'm so sorry."

"Me too," he said.

He must have realized he had been squeezing her fingers because he let them go and rubbed his hands over his thighs.

"Mrs. Winters had always been like a grandmother to me. She treated me just like she treated Jeffery. And since, at the time, my grandparents lived on the East Coast, I embraced that. So, every month I take her to lunch, just as I would have hoped Jeffery would have. She scolds me, gives me advice, and makes me appreciate every single day of my life."

"Carson, that's beautiful."

"A lesson learned at a very high cost."

Abigail took her napkin from the table and dabbed her eyes. "Well, I feel like we're friends now. Thank you for sharing your story with me."

Carson gave her a slow nod and a moment later smiled again. "So, friend, tomorrow night? Will you have dinner with me?"

She certainly had nothing to lose now, she thought. She knew deep in her heart this was the man she was going to marry, just as the premonition had said. Only now, knowing the fate of Mrs. Winters, her heart broke even more. Was she strong enough to see him through that?

"Okay, friend, I'll have dinner with you."

The sadness seemed to lift from his eyes. Once again, those dark eyes looked into her soul.

CHAPTER 10

*A*bigail looked at herself in the little mirror they kept by the back door of the kitchen. She had taken a change of clothes in the makeup bag to work with her that day so that she could change before her date.

"I've never seen you primp this much for anything," Clare said, perched upon the stool at the worktable. "You can't fool me by telling me you're only friends. After all, you've already told me you were going to marry the man."

"I'm still not sure about that. I can't imagine our ideals are going to line up. But I'm not going to lie," Abigail said as she brushed a hand down the front of her skirt. "When I look into those dark eyes, I get a little lost."

"It figures that you'd get the guy. Here I've been in this town twice as long as you have, and nothing. Oh well," she moaned as she hopped down from the stool. "I guess if I really wanted one I should go look for one right?"

Abigail laughed. "Just remember we're both in the same boat. I'm not actually seeing him, yet. I'm not married to him either."

"Call me if you need me. Don't take him home. Call me when you get home."

"Yes, ma'am," she said sternly to her cousin who grinned back at her. "I'm going to be okay."

"I think you will be too. I'll see you in the morning." Clare grabbed her purse and headed out the door.

A moment later the door opened again, and Abigail walked out to the front of the store. Oh, she figured she was a goner. There stood Carson Stone. His dark suit jacket hung open, but his tie was still tied. In his arms, he carried the biggest bouquet of red roses Abigail had ever seen.

She walked toward him. "Are you trying to impress me?"

"Is it working?" He handed her the bouquet.

Abigail sniffed at the petals, and the scent filled her with pleasure. She lifted her eyes to his, and at that moment she saw the same image she saw when Mrs. Winters had touched her hand. This man who stood before her, gazing down at her just as he was. Her heart raced so fast she had to rest her hand on her chest. Dating someone meant you started to get to know them. But what was supposed to happen when one of the people in this newly forming relationship already knew the result? And what if, looking up into his eyes, she knew how much she was going to love him?

"I think it worked."

There was an awkward silence that brewed between them. Deep inside, Abigail wished he would move in and kiss her, but her reaction from the day before probably stopped him. Should give him credit for holding back.

"Let me put these in some water." She turned and walked back to the kitchen, and he followed, just as she hoped he might. "There is a large vase on the top shelf," she said as she pointed up in the storage area. "Would you mind pulling it down?"

"Sure."

Abigail watched, with some delight, as Carson took down the vase. He set it down next to the sink where she had placed the flowers.

"I'll arrange these in the morning. They're going to look beautiful on the front counter."

Carson reached up and tucked a piece of hair behind her ear. The movement so intimate, Abigail had to pay attention to her knees so they wouldn't give out.

"Is your car here?"

"Yes, of course."

That smile, oh that smile, formed on his mouth. "Since I'll be bringing you back here, after dinner, why don't you take them home with you."

"But I'll only be home to sleep. I'm coming right back here in the morning."

"Then I'll get you more roses. I want those to be set next to your bed when you wake up in the morning. I'm trying to make sure I'm the first thing you think about when you wake up."

Abigail swallowed hard. "I thought we were going to dinner as friends."

"Sometimes the best lover starts out as a friend."

She could hardly breathe now. It took everything she had not to throw her arms around Carson's neck and pull him in. Tyrant, she reminded herself. It would be much better if she just kept in mind that he was a tyrant. Perhaps if she could get him to not tear down the church, she could change her mind. Because right at the moment, she really wanted to change her mind.

CARSON HAD MADE RESERVATIONS AT THE GOLDEN HOTEL FOR dinner. He figured it was close. And if for any reason she walked out on him in the middle of dinner, she wouldn't have too far to go. He still wasn't sure the roses had impressed her. Though, there were a few times he thought if he kissed her she'd accept it. Not tonight. He was going to take this nice and slow.

He decided not to tell her how ecstatic Mrs. Winters was that he was taking her to dinner tonight. If it were up to Mrs.

Winters, he'd be proposing tonight. No, he'd never run off and get married as she had. Though something about Abigail tugged at him. Maybe someday he'd run off with her. Okay, it wouldn't be running off. It would be a drawn-out relationship. Watching the way she studied the menu, he figured she'd need a lot of wedding planning. Perhaps even, a lot of encouragement to want to get married. The thought humored him, and he chuckled.

She lowered her menu. "Did I do something funny?"

"Not at all. I'm enjoying watching you make this decision. Have you not eaten here before?"

Abigail put the menu down. "No. I usually work through lunch and breakfast. I'm very frugal. So I often eat at home. And," she began, as she picked up her menu, "I sound like a snob. I'm sorry."

She lifted the menu up to hide her face. How endearing, Carson thought. "I certainly don't take you as a snob. I peg you as somebody who is very thoughtful, and doesn't make rash and spur of the moment decisions."

Lowering the menu, Abigail looked up at him. "I like your analogy much better. I can't make up my mind." She closed the menu and set it down. "I'm going to do something a little bit rash. I'm going to let you decide what I'm eating for dinner."

"You're going to let me decide? I have very good taste."

"I don't eat fish. Make your selection accordingly." She smiled at him, and it twisted him up inside. Yeah, it was going to take a lot of discipline to not pull her to him and kiss her madly. Oh, but when he did, it was going to be magic.

THE CHILL IN THE OCTOBER AIR WAS WELCOME AGAINST ABIGAIL'S skin as they walked from the hotel the two blocks to her shop. Tourists walked the streets and ducked in and out of restaurants and bars. During the summer, when the sun stayed out longer, people dined on the patios of those restaurants and rafted down the creek. It was a tranquil and beautiful place, Abigail thought. She could see herself growing old in the community.

As they turned the corner and she looked up at the mountain, the M glowed from its top. She had quickly learned that the M belonged to the School of Mines which occupied most of downtown Golden. It was like a calling card. But to her, no matter where she was in the city, she knew that right below that M was home.

"That is one of the most beautiful sights I've ever seen," she said glancing toward Carson whose head was down as he walked. "Don't you think?"

His walk slowed, and he finally lifted his eyes. Then he stopped. "Don't think I'm crazy, okay, but I stopped looking at that mountain thinking it was a beautiful sight a long time ago. I only go up there now when I need to clear my head."

Abigail studied him. Who would stop looking at a mountain— and then it dawned on her. Lookout Mountain stood right in front of them. Golden was centered at the base of that very mountain.

She reached for his hand and squeezed it, just as she had when he told her the story. "That was insensitive of me. I didn't think about it."

He turned her toward him and lifted his hand to her cheek. "How could you possibly think that was insensitive? It's a mountain. For me to think it didn't exist, well, that was just silly. In fact, you have no idea how much it helped me to tell you that story. Keeping close with Mrs. Winters, that keeps him alive to me. But in fact, this whole town should keep him alive. We ran amok like crazy kids," he chuckled. He reached for her other hand and clasped their fingers together. "I think of him more fondly now. I think of those good times. Not that one unfortunate one that took him away. Thank you for showing me the beauty in what is around us."

She opened her mouth to say something and then closed it. What else could she say?

They held hands as they walked the last few feet toward her shop.

"I'm going to go inside and get the flowers."

"I'll wait right here for you," he offered as he tucked his hands into his pockets.

Abigail opened the door to the shop and turned on the light. She took a moment and breathed in deep to calm herself. She pushed the word tyrant back into the forefront of her head. She had told Clare she had a mission, she just wasn't sure she believed in it anymore.

Abigail picked up the vase of roses and walked back to the front door where Carson waited.

"Would you hold these for me please," she asked as she handed him the flowers. She locked the door and turned back to him.

"Where's your car?"

"Right behind the building. I can make it to my car."

"I'll carry them to your car. They're very special roses you know," he said, as they went around the building.

"Very special? And what makes them so very special?" she asked as she unlocked the car and opened the door.

Carson handed her the vase, and she belted it carefully into the seat, then she turned back to him for her answer.

"Those came out of Mrs. Winters' garden."

Abigail looked at the roses and then back at Carson. "It's October. Nobody's roses look like that. Now you're telling me stories."

Carson held up his hands as if in surrender. "I kid you not. She has a garden out front, and one in the back. And she has an entire greenhouse of roses that stay beautiful all year."

"Carson, they're beautiful. Tell her how grateful I am that she gave these to you. I will put them next to my bed so that the first thing I think about is you."

He held her gaze. But he didn't move in to kiss her.

"How about tomorrow, you and I stop by her house after work. I know she would love to see you. She is looking very forward to her birthday tea, and the invitation is still open for you to join us."

"Tomorrow I'll be done by six. Pick me up then?"

"See you tomorrow. Now get in your car. I'm not going to walk away until I've seen you drive away."

With a smile, Abigail closed the passenger door and walked around to the other side of the car. "Would you believe it if I told you I've never had a high tea for my birthday?"

"Then consider our invitation. It could be the first of many wonderful things."

She let the words settle around her heart, then climbed into her car, started the engine, and drove away.

CHAPTER 11

*T*he table in the boardroom was covered in blueprints, and that gave Carson some extreme satisfaction. The drawings were for the church on Ford Street. The majority of the building was going to have to come down. Much of it couldn't be saved, structurally. He was glad the blueprints came through before the meeting. Not that it would change the minds of anyone who was going to be there. Perhaps if they saw that they were going to leave the integrity of what was left, they'd be a bit more supportive.

Doug, the architect, began to roll up the blueprints and put them back in their tube. "The area is going to be fantastic. It's too bad you have to go through what you have to go through to get that far."

"It's all part of the process. But what would our freedoms matter if we couldn't chain ourselves to trees that were going to get cut down?"

"Your attitude is better than mine," Doug said as he secured the lid on the tube. "I suppose I'd be the guy ramming the tree with the bulldozer."

Carson wasn't so sure about that, but every once in a while he

63

understood the feeling. What they were planning was going to bring revenue to the area. The church, had it still been a house of worship, would've brought value to the community as well. But the building, vacant for nearly thirty years, was going to bring nothing but tragedy.

Regardless, the threats would still come. The building would be built. He'd move onto the next project. Today, however, he had a date with two amazing women. One he knew nearly as well as he knew himself, the other he felt he might if she'd spend more time with him.

As Doug cleaned up his things and left the room, Carson leaned back in his chair and chewed on the end of his pen. He had never met anyone quite like Abigail. There were times when she looked at him, and he thought she could read him. Other times, he thought perhaps she was afraid of him.

He'd been brainstorming about her birthday. Mrs. Winters was easy. She wanted to have tea. What could he do for Abigail that would make her birthday special? He'd give it some thought. Perhaps he'd ask his mother. She seemed to be in good with Abigail. That would be a good thing, wouldn't it? If they got married, and his mother liked her?

Carson sat forward and put his feet on the floor. He'd gone lightheaded just thinking about it. He'd never thought of any of the women he'd dated like that. Marriage had never crossed his mind.

Sure, he assumed someday he get married. He didn't figure he'd start making plans in his own head about a woman he'd only met a few weeks ago. He supposed when the time was right, the time was right. Mrs. Winters would probably agree with him there.

Carson sucked in a breath and let it out slowly. He was lucky he managed a dinner date last night. He'd see how it went when they went to visit Mrs. Winters today. Perhaps after they had their visit, he could convince her to take a stroll down alongside

Clear Creek. Carson always thought himself charming under the moonlight.

The thought made him laugh, and he stood up and returned to his office.

⁓

THE HIGH TEA FOR THURSDAY AFTERNOON HAD BEEN FULLY reserved. Abigail had found that most of the tourists came in on Thursday afternoons, and tea was an easy enough outing for them. Most of them had plans to head to the mountains, climb a fourteener, and tour the brewery. Golden was filling up with microbreweries, and that alone had become a massive fascination to the tourists who frequented Golden.

Abigail was clearing an empty table, her hands full of antique Prussian cups when Carson strolled through the door. She looked up at him, a panic zipped through her heart. "You're extremely early. Nothing happened to Mrs. Winters did it?"

Had his face flashed a sign of annoyance? "No, I spoke to her half an hour ago, she's fine. I wrapped up early and thought I would come here. If I'm in the way…"

"No. No, I'm sorry. Can I get you a cup of tea? We have some fresh scones."

He moved to her and took the cups from her hand. "Let me help you. If Clare is okay with it, I'll sit in the back. I'll be like the very special friend who just gets to hang out in the kitchen," he said with a wink as he turned toward the kitchen.

Abigail brushed her hands down the front of her apron. She supposed she should get used to that. If all of her premonitions came true, he'd probably be sitting in the kitchen quite a bit. She pressed a hand to her jittery stomach. She wasn't sure if she got nervous around him because she knew their fate, or if she was beginning to feel their fate. Still, she had a plan. First things first; to save that church. She would just have to push aside her feelings for Carson until that had happened. If this burden of a superpower was going to inhibit how she lived her life, she might as well use it for good. She was absolutely sure he would want to be with her. So she was going to get her way.

She turned back to the table and picked up a few more dishes and scraped the crumbs from the table. Yes, she'd make him a warm scone and a cup of tea. She'd visit his lifelong friend, and perhaps tonight he would finally kiss her. She could go along with that. That church would be saved by the end of the week.

By the time she had taken the dishes to the kitchen, Clare had already set Carson up with a cup of tea and a scone.

"She's packing up a box of scones and pastries for Mrs. Winters."

"Good," Abigail said. "I had wanted to do that for her. I think she'll enjoy it."

"Oh, she will. She keeps talking about it. I told her she should come down and see you anytime, but I think she's afraid of leaving home by herself."

Abigail caught the look that Clare shot toward her. "Her husband isn't living any longer?"

"He died years ago. So, even though we have lunch every month, I make sure to stop by every couple days. Her kids are nearby too, as well as her grandkids. But, I happen to be the closest."

Abigail turned so that he couldn't see her, and neither could Clare. A few moments ago she wanted to use the man to get what she needed. But how could she do that to somebody whose heart was so big? The struggle inside of her burned. "Let me finish cleaning up the front area. I think I will be done here soon. Then we can head over."

"Take your time," he said picking up his scone and taking a bite. "I'm in no hurry, and I forgot to eat lunch. I may have to scam another scone from Clare."

Clare laughed, and brought him another one, setting it on his plate.

Well, Abigail thought, he'd already won her over, and she'd been as mad about the church as Abigail had been, perhaps more so. She'd take each day one at a time. Right now, however, she wanted to see Mrs. Winters for herself. She was afraid perhaps the illness was already starting to take over.

CHAPTER 12

*M*rs. Winters lived on the back side of Lookout
Mountain in Genesee. Abigail wondered if
perhaps it was too big a house for her, and too far from anyone
else. Sure, she had plenty of neighbors, but still, they weren't
right next door.

Carson put the car in park in the driveway. "Let me open your
door," he said. "I would do it anyway. I think it's a gentlemanly
thing to do. But if she's looking out the window, and she sees you
get out without me opening your door, I'll be in a lot of trouble."

Abigail laughed. "I promise not to make you look bad in front
of her. Is that her front yard rose garden?"

Carson followed her gaze to the front door. "Yep. And it's
early October, don't they look great?"

"They do. My mother would be very jealous. She has a rose
garden, but it's nothing in comparison." She laughed again. "In
fact, it's just a garden full of thorns."

"I'd like to see that sometime," he said and climbed from
the car.

Abigail let that linger. Did he really want to go home with

69

her? Perhaps not right away. After all, people still thought she was strange. They might try to sway him in different directions.

He opened the door and held out his hand. Abigail took it and stepped out of the car just as Mrs. Winters opened the front door.

"Good afternoon, Mrs. Winters," Abigail called up to her.

"Abigail, how wonderful to see you. Carson, you help her up the stairs," she instructed, and Carson offered his arm.

He'd been right. She looked frailer. As Abigail reached the top stair, Mrs. Winters held out her hand to her. Abigail prayed that the look of fear didn't take over her face, but she was sincerely afraid to touch her. She didn't want to know the truth behind her illness. But she took the woman's hand, and kept a gracious smile on her face as the world around her spun, flickered light, and embedded images so deep in her mind, she'd never get them out.

She felt Carson's hand come to her waist. He moved in close. "Are you okay?" He whispered in her ear. "You look like you did the other day."

"I'm fine. The altitude still gets to me sometimes."

They followed Mrs. Winter back to her kitchen. Abigail smiled when she saw the display that she had set out on the table. There would be no need for them to go to dinner tonight, she thought. Mrs. Winters obviously knew how to entertain.

"Abigail, I'm so glad you came to my home. I would still like it if you would have tea with us for my birthday."

Carson nudged her with his elbow. "I told you."

Mrs. Winters urged them both to sit, and she sat with them. Abigail noted that she was winded by the time they sat down.

"I love your home here. The scenery is beautiful."

Mrs. Winters instructed Carson to begin to serve them. "Where are you from, Abigail?"

Abigail took the small plate that Carson held out to her. "Just outside Kansas City. My family still lives there."

"My husband and I would travel there often. I have family there too. All of Carson's people are here. Isn't that right, Carson?"

He had stood to pour them each a glass of lemonade. "That's correct."

Abigail thought she'd be more comfortable if she directed the conversation toward him. "Tell me about your family, Carson."

There was a moment of shock that registered on his face. And, by Mrs. Winter's smile, she recognized it as well.

Carson sat down and placed the pitcher of lemonade in front of him. "You've met my mother. I assume it won't be long before you meet my father. She's already talked to him about you, and wanting to take him to your store. I have an older sister who lives in Boulder with her husband and three kids. My brother lives in Denver with his wife. They don't have any kids, and right now they're living the LoDo life."

Mrs. Winters touched Abigail's arm again. "His family is fantastic. You want to get to know them," she said as if she had all the information she was transferring to Abigail.

Abigail warmly smiled. "I hate to interrupt getting to know everybody, but may I use your restroom?"

"Of course, it's right down the hall," she offered as she pointed in the direction.

Abigail noted that Carson stood as she left the room.

She quickly found the restroom and tucked herself inside. She let out a long steady breath. The Alzheimer's, though Mrs. Winters seemed very sharp at the moment, was rapidly taking over. She didn't suppose by Christmas that Mrs. Winters would be living in the same house. Her heart ached, so she pressed her hand to it.

And Carson, she and Carson—oh, it took her breath away. If the images were correct, she and Carson would be married on the hillside where she assumed Jeffery died. She saw a tiny house, three small children, and herself with a pregnant belly. It was more vivid than anything she'd ever seen in her entire life, and that included the girl in the river. But there had been something else. She could hardly breathe. It had been dark, dusty, and it was if it was all falling in around her. Carson was there too. There was no need to fight this anymore, Carson was her soulmate. This relationship was meant to be, to grow, to endure. Perhaps she needed to come out and be straightforward with him. That would be best. It would give them an opportunity to run, run like hell. She'd consider doing that. Not tonight. Maybe not tomorrow. But soon. In fact for the next few weeks, she figured she'd be giving Carson some strength. He was going to need it with Mrs. Winters' deterioration. Abigail swore to herself that she would have tea with them. It would be an honor to be served tea along with Mrs. Winters.

AFTER WHAT HAD BEEN AN ABSOLUTELY BEAUTIFUL AFTERNOON, Carson drove back to town and parked outside the tea shop. He turned off the engine and sat there quietly. Abigail didn't move. Perhaps she was afraid to get out of the car without him opening the door. He shifted a glance in her direction.

"Her son called me today. He told me she's in the early stages of Alzheimer's. I haven't been able to wrap my head around that."

"It's a rapid-moving disease. She'll be very lucky to have you around."

"I'm not ready to watch that happen."

Abigail reached across the car and took his hand, holding it tight. "Don't ask me how, but I knew she was sick. Her sickness is going to take over. You need to talk to her family, and they need to put her in a home soon. For her own good."

He looked at her, narrowing his eyes. "Don't tell me not to ask, that's a lot of information."

"In time. Please trust me."

He kept his eyes locked onto hers. It was as if he'd been looking into her eyes his whole life, she knew him. It was all too strange. Why her? Why now?

On instinct, and as if it was the most natural thing to do, he leaned in and pressed his lips to hers.

CHAPTER 13

*A*bigail's first reaction would have been to pull back, but Carson's mouth on hers felt right. She'd never been kissed like that before. Every emotion she'd ever had swirled inside of her. She wanted to pull him closer, but there was a great need to push him away. Instead, she stayed with him, his mouth moving against hers, his hand reaching up into her hair.

It was love. It was absolute love rushing right at her. She had to tell him the truth. He had to know she saw this coming, both him and Mrs. Winters. He would run. He would run fast and far. They all did.

She pulled back and caught her breath.

Carson eased back in his seat. "I'm sorry. I promised myself I would wait a long time before I did that. I couldn't wait any longer."

"Don't apologize. I wanted you to do that. I just think it's going to make things difficult."

"Why should it be difficult? We're getting to know each other. I didn't ask you to marry me."

She pulled her keys from her purse and held them in her hand. No, she was sure she understood how he would propose to her. It hadn't been a full premonition, but there were pieces. She damned this sixth sense. She hated that it stole all the special moments of her life. Although, the premonitions hadn't come from him, except that one dark one. They'd all come from Mrs. Winters.

"I should get headed home. Clare is taking the morning off tomorrow. I need to be in early." She opened the car door. "You don't need to help me out of the car. I'll be fine."

But as she stepped out onto the sidewalk, he opened his door and walked around to her. In a matter of seconds, she found herself wrapped in his arms and pressed against him again. She looked up into dark brown eyes, and at that moment she felt total calm.

"Don't walk away from me upset, please. If I've moved too fast, I'm sorry. There is simply something about you, and it pulls me to you."

"I've never had anybody attracted to me before," she said looking down.

Carson lifted her chin with his finger. "I don't believe that. Everything about you is perfect."

She winced, and her heart ached with his words. "That's proof you don't know anything about me."

"That's why I'm begging for a chance to get to know you. If you're not interested, you need to tell me. But I'm the kind of guy that asks questions. I'm gonna want to know why."

She was interested. Regardless of knowing their fate, he had piqued her interest. "I am interested," she said as she ran a hand down his arm and thought how nice it was to be wrapped up in them. "Give me time."

"I have all the time in the world," he promised as he dipped his head to kiss her again.

This time she let herself sink with the kiss. Raising her arms, she wrapped them around his neck and pulled him in tightly. The kiss warmed her, from her head to her toes. Perhaps this would be the best birthday gift she'd ever given herself, a chance to love someone and let them love her. If he truly did love her, in time, he'd understand her gift—her burden.

Carson's fingers tangled in her hair as his tongue moved between her lips. Abigail was quite sure if she died right then, she would die a happy woman.

As Carson pulled back, he brushed her cheek with his thumb. "I'll come by tomorrow after work. Let's go for a walk down by Clear Creek. I'll try to take it slow, and simple. But it'll kill me until I see you again, even if it is tomorrow."

"I'll see you then," she said she pulled away slowly and walked around the building towards her car.

MEETINGS, BLUEPRINTS, AND AGENDAS WERE PART OF CARSON'S usual day. Because he was addicted to his work, each one of those items always brought some joy to him. But today, his mind was a million miles away. All he could think about was Abigail.

He thought of her voice, her clothes, and how her hair felt between his fingers. He closed his eyes and thought of the kisses, so soft, and so warm.

Moving his chair closer to his desk, he opened up his computer. He typed the name of her tea store into the search bar just to see a picture of it. Scanning through the menu, the history, and the reviews made him feel as though he were with her.

Clicking the About Us tab, he brought up a picture of Clare and Abigail standing outside the tea room in front of the big window with the logo on it. They each had a bio, so he read them.

He knew Abigail had moved here from near Kansas City. So what was it that was near Kansas City? He typed in her name to the search tab, along with the words tea shop, and Kansas City. Then, a whole list of things popped up.

Because he wanted to know who she was when she lived near Kansas City, he started at the bottom and scrolled his way up.

A cheerleader in a small rural high school.

Captain of the debate team.

Honor roll student.

Daughter of a pharmacist, who had worked at the local pharmacy for nearly thirty years.

Suspect in the murder of Katie Meadows, ten-year-old, fifth-grader who had been found drowned in the river.

That last headline had him stopping, his hand forming to the mouse on his desk. Obviously, the name Abigail Weston was common enough to get honor roll students, cheerleaders, and murderers all bunched together in a search engine.

However, it was curious enough that he clicked the link.

Katie Meadows had gone missing on a March evening. The article went on to say that her friends had said they were all going to meet at the elementary school at eleven o'clock at night. It was all a matter of testing boundaries at a young age. When Katie did not arrive, they assumed she got scared. It wasn't until nearly ten o'clock the next morning that her parents notified police that she was missing. A search began right away. Katie Meadows was not found until Abigail Weston, daughter of Mr. and Mrs. Clyde Weston of Parkville, Missouri, came forth suggesting that they look downriver for Katie Meadows. The body of the missing fifth-grader was found in the White Branch River.

Abigail Weston was held for questioning; however, after further investigation, the girl's death was ruled an accidental death. No more information was given on how Ms. Weston obtained the information as to where to find the body.

Carson rubbed his fingers over his chin as he read the article over and over. He was immersed enough in his investigation, that when his mother opened his office door, it startled him.

"You must be working really hard." His mother walked further into his office. "I knocked. I promise I did."

"Sorry, I was reading something."

"I was just going to tell you that I was going to leave a little early today. Your father and I are going over to Abigail's store for lunch. A late lunch. I want him to meet her," she said enthusiastically.

Carson only nodded. The story still had him emotionally twisted up. He'd ask her about it tonight. Perhaps, nearby Kansas City had more than one Abigail Weston. Yes, that had to be it.

Carson closed the computer and looked up at his mother. "I took Abigail over to Mrs. Winter's house yesterday. It was a nice visit," he said as his mother fidgeted with items on his desk. "Her son called, she's in the early stages of Alzheimer's."

His mother's hands stopped fidgeting. "Carson, that's horrible."

"It is. I'm also dating Abigail," he interjected.

His mother had grown silent, and her mouth dropped open. "Carson, that's a lot to drop on me all at once."

"I know, I didn't mean to do that."

"I'm happy for you. I'm truly happy for you." She pressed her hands to her chest. "My heart aches for Mrs. Winters. But I want to be happy for you. Know that I'm happy for you."

"I know. You and dad go and have a nice afternoon. I'm stopping by there after work. I have some more work to do on the Ford Street church. But tell her I say hello."

The smile returned to his mother's face. "Will you let Mrs. Winters know I'm thinking of her, and tell her that I'll come to visit soon."

Carson stood and walked around his desk. He pulled his mother into a warm hug. "I'll let her know. She does love your company."

His mother patted his cheek and then left his office.

Carson sat back down at his desk and opened his computer. In the search bar he typed the death of Katie Meadows.

CHAPTER 14

*A*bigail and Clare hovered in the kitchen, peering out the doorway. At the corner table, Patricia and Al Stone sat having a late lunch.

"His mother brought his father here to meet me," she said shaking her head. "What have I gotten myself into?"

"According to your premonition, you didn't get yourself into this. It's fate. It's meant to be. Just think about it, you're gonna save that old church."

Clare went back to finalizing the trays for the next day.

Abigail moved to the prep table and sat on the stool. "He has a community meeting next week about the church. I'm trying to decide how to bring it up before then. I think it would be better if he just changed his mind before people started to attack him."

"Like me?"

Abigail took the pile of newly laundered napkins and began to fold them. "Well, you were very vocal at the last meeting."

"Yeah, that's what those meetings are for. We the people do not want the church torn down."

"I know. I don't want to see it destroyed either. I'm just not sure this short relationship we've had justifies me telling him what to do."

"You're going to marry him."

"So says that stupid premonition that I had. What if I'm wrong? What if I really don't have a sixth sense and I'm just being silly."

Clare stopped what she was doing and fisted her hands on her hips. "You've never been wrong. You knew when grandma was sick. You knew that Mrs. Winters was sick. You saw things were going to happen to Carson, you got him out of harm's way. Even if it was just to tell him to stop by and grab a box of pastries. You know damn good and well you're going to get married, and have four kids."

"And I hate everything about that premonition," she argued with her cousin. "I don't want to know that this is the man I'm going to marry. I want it all to be a wonderful surprise."

"Well, maybe this is a premonition just for Mrs. Winters. You still haven't seen anything when you touched him. Or kissed him. Maybe you'll see something when you..."

Abigail shot up her hand. "Stop. Let's not go there."

Clare shrugged her hands in the air. "He seems like a nice enough man, minus the fact that he tears down perfectly good buildings. His parents seem good. Hell, even his best eighty-year-old friend seems good. Maybe you should go sit with them," she said as she nodded towards Carson's parents. "Take the opportunity to get to know them. Maybe you can stop the demolition of that building through them."

Abigail shook her head as she climbed off the stool. "I'm not going to use them."

"Oh, but you knew you were going marry Carson, and you're willing to use him?"

Abigail let out a breath of frustration. Fate could be changed. Of course it could be. There was no reason to think that Carson Stone was actually going to be her forever after. Although, just thinking about the kiss they'd shared, she wouldn't mind that forever.

She took a pitcher of water and carried it out to the Stones' table. "Can I get you anything else?"

Patricia looked up at her lovingly, just as Abigail assumed she looked up at her son. "Abigail, please pull up a chair and sit for just a moment. I want Al to get to know you."

She wanted to refuse. However, she set down the pitcher of water, pulled over a chair, and sat with Carson's parents.

What had Carson told them that made them want to come in today? Had he told them about going out and about kissing her? Was he a kiss-and-tell kind of guy? What better way to get to know somebody than to sit with their parents.

"Mr. Stone, what do you do for a living?" Abigail asked.

"I'm a retired architect. I did a lot of business in downtown Denver. Before this big boom of course. I think that's why Carson is interested in the development of new things. He always saw me working at my draft table, and would join me."

That was good to know. His father must not have appreciated old things either.

Patricia put her hand over Abigail's, and suddenly Abigail's entire body began to vibrate with a pulse she never felt before.

"I'm so glad that Carson took you to see Mrs. Winters yesterday. He told me about her condition. It's dreadful. She's been like a grandmother to him. I'm sure he told you about her grandson, about him dying?"

Abigail could only nod. The buzzing in her ears was horrific.

Patricia removed her hand and picked up her sandwich. "I'm going to go see her tomorrow. Perhaps I could take her some lemon cake."

Abigail forced a smile to her face. "I'll go get one boxed up for her. On the house. It brings me great joy to think that she would enjoy it."

Before she could turn away, Patricia called after her. "Carson told me you share a birthday with Mrs. Winters. Isn't that amazing? I think it was fate that you came here. I'm so very happy that you did."

Again, Abigail smiled and turned away. What had he told them? As far as his mother should be concerned so far, she was just somebody who owned his shop where Carson frequented. A dinner and a kiss, that shouldn't say forever to his mother. Was he that desperate a man?

Abigail boxed up a small loaf of lemon bread and tied a beautiful pink ribbon around it. At that moment, she wished she had a rose to tuck into the ribbon.

As Mr. and Mrs. Stone rose to leave, the front door opened. Abigail walked out of the kitchen, the loaf of lemon bread in her hands, and noticed Carson walking in the door. Patricia moved to him immediately and threw her arms around him, embracing him as a giddy mother would. His father shook his hand and patted him on the shoulder.

When he noticed her, he gave her a quick glance, and then looked away. His eyes were dark—angry dark. He must've had a bad day. She certainly wasn't going to mention the Ford Street church now.

Handing Mrs. Stone the box, she said, "give Mrs. Winters my best. Tell her I'm looking forward to our birthday tea."

Carson looked at her again and gave her a nod, which she assumed meant he agreed.

A moment later his parents left the store, and she was standing awkwardly alone with Carson near the counter.

"Can I get you something to eat? Or something to drink? You're off work early aren't you?"

Carson ran his hand over the back of his neck and moved his head from side to side as if to work out the kinks that might have settled there. "Can I get a glass of water? You wouldn't have any Tylenol would you?"

"Sure, are you not feeling well?"

"I'm fine. What time are you done tonight?"

"I have two more high teas. Then we're done for the afternoon."

He followed her to the back where he said hello to Clare. Abigail retrieved a glass of water for him, and the Tylenol.

"Thanks," he said as he swallowed back the pills. "Do you like sushi?"

"I've never had more than a California roll from the grocery store."

"There's a great little place over on South Golden Road. I'll pick you up when you're done and take you to dinner. I have something I wanted to talk to you about."

Abigail's heart began to hammer in her chest. What could he possibly want to talk about? "That sounds delightful."

"Text me when you're ready to leave. I'll swing by." He gave Clare a wave, and Abigail a thoughtful look. He didn't hug her, and he didn't try to kiss her either. Then, he turned and walked out of the store.

Clare moved in and stood next to Abigail as they both watched him walk out to his car and drive away. "That was really weird."

"I know. I don't know what to expect."

"Maybe he's going to tell you that it won't work."

"Why spend money on sushi then? He could've told me right here."

Clare nodded in agreement. "You're too practical. I would've just started getting mad."

What was there to get mad about? Then again, what had his eyes so dark and worrisome? She supposed she'd find out soon enough. For now, she needed to serve her guests as the next set walked in the door.

CHAPTER 15

*C*arson drove around town for the next hour. Up Lookout Mountain, and back down. He'd even driven by Mrs. Winters' house, though he didn't go inside. The name Katie Meadows kept swirling in his head. Abigail did not seem like the kind of person who would be involved in anybody's disappearance or murder. Would she answer him when he asked her about it? Would this be a turning point?

He wasn't ready to give up yet. There was something deep inside of him that told him to fight for this. He supposed it would depend on how she reacted when he brought up the name. Should he do that during dinner? Perhaps he should wait until they were alone. He didn't take Abigail as the cause a scene type; however, you never knew with women.

He returned to the tea shop just as the lights went off. Good timing, he thought. Carson climbed from his car and walked across the street. He gently knocked on the door, which was locked, and watched as Abigail walked from the kitchen to the door.

"Great timing. Clare just left, and we just closed out. Pretty good day for Wednesday." She gathered her purse and her keys.

"After you left I looked up sushi restaurants on South Golden Road. There's only one. So I looked at the menu. I think I can safely say there's plenty of stuff to order," she said enthusiastically as they walked through the front door and she locked it behind her. "Do you do the raw stuff? I've never been able to understand that."

"Yeah. I do."

They walked across the street to his car, and he opened the door for her. She gave him a gentle smile as if she noticed he was short and to the point. He needed to shake this mood, or he was never going to get any information from her.

Carson walked around the other side of the car and slid in behind the driver seat. He sat for a moment. "What kind of music do you like?"

Her eyes went wide, and she thought for a moment. "My mother loves country music. My father is heavy-metal. I never could quite grasp either side. I like jazz. Well, and contemporary. I'm not much into hip-hop and certainly not into rap."

The description was enough to make him chuckle, and ease up a bit. He scanned through the XM channels on the radio and stopped at a jazz station. "How is this?"

"Nice. What did you have it on before?"

"Business Journal talk radio. I didn't think it was going to set quite the mood."

She sat back in her seat and smiled. "I appreciate the change then."

They drove in silence to the restaurant. Abigail didn't often eat out, so spending time with a nice-looking man who was willing to take her out, had its perks.

The man who sat them called Carson by name and even gave him a hefty pat on the back. He ordered them each a glass of wine and began to fill out his order on the sushi menu.

"The menu has cooked items," he said obviously noticing she was studying the sushi menu too hard.

"I should step out of my comfort zone, right?"

"The fact that I've dined with you more than once says I've crossed into a comfort zone of sorts. The first time we met I got the distinct impression you might not like me too much."

Abigail set down the menu. "I think I would like a tempura meal."

Carson finished his order and set it to the side. He studied her. "I'm right. You didn't like me."

What was she supposed to say that? She supposed the right thing to do would to be honest. "When I first met you, you were charming. You were the perfect gentleman around Mrs. Winters. I assumed she was your grandmother, and you were being very polite. It wasn't until I read your name on your credit card that I knew who you were."

"And you recognized my name?"

"Of course. Then I remembered I'd seen it before."

"Because you went to the community meeting about the Ford Street church."

She felt her breath sticking in her lungs. Picking up her wine, she sipped to moisten her dry mouth. "You saw me there?"

He shook his head. "Not really. I remembered Clare."

Abigail winced. "She was very vocal."

"People who are adamant about something usually are vocal. Everyone's entitled to their own opinion."

This wasn't actually how she imagined they would get into this conversation. But she supposed it was as perfect a time as any.

"And you're adamant about changing the footprint of the city?"

His eyes went wider and she noticed his jaw tightened. "The building is old, empty, and dangerous. I'm curious, what would you do with it?"

Abigail took a breath and then swallowed it. Her mind had gone blank. She hadn't thought she'd be faced with the question like that. "The history of Colorado isn't too old. You have to admit that. You won't find many buildings that are over two-hundred years old."

"You're right," he said leaning his arms on the table. "But you didn't answer my question. What would you do with the building?"

Abigail searched her mind to think of something. "It's big enough for a brewery."

Carson nodded. "There are over a hundred and forty micro-brewers in Colorado. Let me count how many are in Golden," he said in a tone that had her fighting back a curse.

"Fine. We certainly don't need another brewery in town. I get it." She realized she could name at least four of them within a mile radius of her tea shop. That didn't include Coors. "What about another church? Why would a..."

"To keep the structural integrity of the building, it would cost nearly two million dollars. Do you know a church that has two million?"

She wasn't a fan of this game. "I feel as though I'd do better if I had some research."

"Look it up online. Everything has full disclosure. And, if you want to come see the plans, feel free."

Straightening her back, clasping her hands in her lap, she steadied her breath. "I just might do that. I just don't see a reason to tear down such an amazing building."

Carson shrugged as the waitress set their tray in front of them full of beautiful sushi and tempura. He picked up his chopsticks and a piece of yellowtail. "If Golden were to get one tiny little earthquake, I wouldn't have a reason to tear down either. The building is so unstable it would just collapse."

As she had not heard of any earthquakes in recent times in

Colorado, she thought that was a horrible excuse. "Well, then I'm guessing it will stay up until I get my research done."

Dinner conversation had come to a strange halt. Though they didn't say much, she realized how comfortable she was with him in silence. That usually didn't happen unless you knew somebody well. And she hardly knew him all.

After dinner, he drove straight back to her shop. As soon as he cut the engine, he stepped out of the car and walked around it to open her door.

"I had a nice evening," she said, but by the small grunt he gave, she wasn't sure he'd had a nice evening. Perhaps she had been too hard on him about the church. That was her mission, right? Then she realized she didn't like how it felt right now. "I'm sorry about what I said at the restaurant. Sorry I got so upset over the building."

"It happens. People don't understand what I do. I'll admit, I hoped you would. Do you have to go back inside the shop?" he asked.

"No."

"I'll wait for you to get your car."

Abigail stood there for another moment, waiting. He didn't touch her hand. Nor did he reach for her or kiss her. Regret surged through her, and she felt horrible now.

"Thank you again."

Carson gave her a curt nod of his head as she headed off to get her car.

CHAPTER 16

The mood Carson was in would sour anybody's milk. He hadn't asked Abigail about Katie Meadows' death, but he certainly got the gist of her disgust for the Ford Street church project. And to top it all off, when he had stopped by Mrs. Winter's house that morning because her son had asked him to, she talked about Jeffery. It wasn't as if she remembered him. It was as if she had spoken to him.

He wasn't ready to face that. He had enough on his plate, and worrying about Mrs. Winters in her declining health, that tore him up.

Emily entered his office with a stack of papers and a cup of coffee.

"You wanted me to remind you that you have a meeting at ten with the zoning commission. Your mother is having lunch catered in for the office. And Abigail Weston is in reception and asked to speak to you."

He watched Emily's face to see if there was any recognition of who Abigail might be. He decided that his mother must not have bought into sharing office gossip. Perhaps she wanted to take him up on the offer to look at the plans. Well, fine. If that's what was important to her, and that's what was important to him.

"Send her in."

Emily handed him a cup of coffee and set the papers on the table in the corner of the room where he would hold private meetings. As she left his office, he took a long sip of coffee to give his blood a little jolt.

Abigail walked into his office, as bright as a ray of sunshine, he thought. Her hair was pulled back in a ponytail, and she wore a bright yellow dress. Her coat was draped over her arm. And though her outfit was bright and welcoming, distress was painted on her face.

Carson stood from behind his desk and moved to her. "Did something happen? I assumed you came to look at the architectural plans for the Ford Street church, but your face says something different."

"I'm sorry to bother you at work," she said picking something off her jacket that he couldn't see. "I just thought it was important enough I should tell you."

So perhaps she had decided to come clean about Katie Meadows, he thought. Good. He'd rather hear her side without having to ask for it.

He reached out and touched her arms, which were cold. "Come sit down. Can I get you some coffee?"

"I can't stay for long. I need to get to work. We have a tour bus coming in, and if I'm not there in time, Clare will lose her mind."

"Okay, what did you need to tell me?"

Abigail chewed on her bottom lip for a moment. "I had a dream last night. I have lots of strange dreams. But this one was at Mrs. Winters'. So I got up early this morning, and went to her house."

"I was at her house this morning. When were you there?"

"Maybe fifteen minutes ago."

"I must have just missed you then."

Abigail nodded. "She said that you had been there." She reached for his hand and gave it a squeeze. "Carson, she starting to fail. You need to convince her family to move her into a home."

"I agree. This morning she was telling me she had been talking to Jeffery."

"Yes, she told me that too. But that's not the part that startles me." She shut her eyes tight and gripped his hand. When she opened her eyes, they affixed on his. "I want you to trust me. I want you to know that I know things, and I'll explain later. I'm afraid if she doesn't get out of the house in the next week, there's going to be a fire."

Carson pulled from Abigail and took a step back to pace. He raked his fingers through his hair and then shoved his hands in his pockets. "Did she say she was going to build a fire? Was she going to cook?"

"I'm asking you to trust me."

Carson rubbed his fingers over his chin. "And here I thought you came to complain about the church again."

He saw the flash of anger in her eyes. "Complain? I came to help. But evidently, you don't want my help. Perhaps you could get in touch with her family."

Carson sucked in a breath. He tripped over the fine line. "I'll go by, make sure she's safe. I'll go through the house, turn off the oven, make sure there are no matches," he said sincerely.

Any other woman this would have been it. To have a woman walking to his office and casually give him information that she couldn't back up, that was cause for thinking she was crazy. But not Abigail. He needed to calm her. He needed to please her. He couldn't let this hang in the air.

Carson moved to her and caressed her cheek with his hand. "I'm sorry I jumped you. I seem to be in a bit of a bad mood."

"Please trust me. I'll explain it all soon."

Abigail moved into him. She pressed her lips to his and

lingered there softly. He breathed in her scent, let the calm of the kiss wash over him.

When she pulled back, her eyes were softer. "Would you like to come over for dinner tonight?"

"To the store?"

Abigail shook her head. "No. Come to my house. I'd like to cook dinner for you."

They made a turn in their new relationship, he decided. They'd had their first argument and the first big kiss. Now she was inviting him to her home. He figured that was a big step. Maybe she'd open up to him there.

"I would love that."

"I'll text you my address. I should be home around seven."

"I'll be there."

She lingered in front of him for just another moment, kissed the tips of her fingers and pressed it to his cheek before she strode out of his office.

Carson backed up and leaned on the top of his desk. He loved her. He thought he had loved others, which he now knew he hadn't, but he loved Abigail Weston. They hadn't gotten to know each other well, hadn't even slept in the same bed, yet he knew. He'd get to the bottom of all his questions. There was time.

He decided he take her warning, and head over to Mrs. Winters' again. What would it hurt to take a look around? As he opened his desk drawer to retrieve his car keys, Emily walked through the door.

"The men from zoning are here in the conference room," Emily informed him.

Where had his morning gone? "I'll be there in a moment." Emily left the office, and Carson gathered his notes. He'd check on Mrs. Winters later.

CHAPTER 17

Once all the high tea reservations had closed out, Abigail left the store. She stopped by the grocery store and gathered her items for the evening, and something for breakfast just in case.

She had no idea what kind of wine he would drink. The man at the liquor store guided her to something that would go with what she was cooking for dinner.

As she set everything out on her counter, she pulled up the text message from Clare with instructions on how to prepare the meal she had planned. Abigail wasn't a fantastic cook, though she would never starve. Clare, on the other hand, was not only fantastic with baking, but an amazing chef.

Abigail turned on some music, wrapped an apron around her waist, and began to cook dinner. She mixed, cut, and chopped, realizing the work was pleasant. Exactly at seven o'clock, there was a knock at the door.

She took a cleansing breath, untied the apron around her waist, and opened the front door.

Standing in front of her, Carson held out a grocery store

bouquet of flowers. "I thought I was going to be late. These are an apology gift, even though I'm on time."

Abigail took the flowers and held them to her chest. "I guess since no apology is necessary, they are a delightfully nice gift."

Carson raised both hands to her cheeks and moved in to kiss her. His lips were warm and inviting. Her heart raced, and her head swam with the kiss. Perhaps she made the right choice to buy breakfast. She was ready to have him in her home.

As he pulled back and studied her for a moment, she noticed the dark circles under his eyes. Had he not been sleeping? Had the awkwardness of their date the night before caused his turmoil?

This was her way of making it up to him. "Can I offer you a glass of wine?"

"I'd like that."

She shut the front door and took his hand. Looking into her kitchen, she wondered what he thought of her little home. She had an inheritance from her grandmother, and when she moved to Colorado, she bought the house. It needed some work, and she'd done some. But what did the developer in him see? Was renovation in his blood?

Taking the bottle, which was open so it could breathe, upon recommendation from the man at the liquor store, she poured each glass. She handed him his glass and held hers as if to toast. "Here's to you coming to my house."

"Here's to the first invitation."

She drank to that, and as she did, she wondered what his house looked like. Assuming he lived in a modern place, she inwardly questioned whether he lived in a condo or townhouse. Was his decor more modern, as hers was eclectic? Did he have a housekeeper, or did he tidy up himself? She'd seen his car and his office, and she assumed he was very fastidious. The number of toiletries on the back of her sink might make him cringe. She supposed she'd find out.

"I just finished dinner. It's ready anytime you are."

He gazed at her, and then a faint smile formed on his lips. "Do you mind if we sit for a few minutes? Enjoy our wine?"

"It's a little chilly, but I have an enclosed patio that looks out over South Table Mountain if you're interested."

"If you sit close enough to me, perhaps it won't be too chilly."

She took his hand again, and let him out the back door to the enclosed patio. There was a small wicker sofa, draped with a blanket, where she often sat and read. Abigail sat down, and Carson followed. She took the blanket and draped it over their legs. "This is my favorite part of the house. Rabbits hop around the yard, and once in a while you see deer grazing right outside."

Carson wound his fingers in her ponytail. "Your home is charming, just like you."

She wondered why when he touched her she didn't see anything of the future. Thinking back to that morning when she had gone to see Mrs. Winters, she had gone to see if the premonition of her and Carson may have been wrong. A week ago she had wished it was. It was interesting that after their first, what she considered a disagreement, she didn't want it to be wrong at all.

The dream she had the night before about the fire must have clouded anything else. When Mrs. Winters had patted her arm, there was an immense sense of calm. No premonition of the fire. No premonition of her and Carson.

Had she not been correct so many times in her life, she would have decided that it was all a mistake. How could a woman who was dying be so calm, especially when she was explaining a conversation she'd had with her dead grandson?

Carson trailed a finger down the side of her neck. She turned to look at him. "What are you thinking?" he asked.

No, she didn't want to tell him what she was thinking. She just wasn't ready yet. "I was wondering what you thought of my house. And, I was wondering what your house looked like."

His hand moved back to her hair. "My house is not as quaint as yours."

"So you have a house?"

"You thought I lived in a condo, didn't you?"

Abigail laughed, then took a sip of her wine. "It was between a condo and a townhouse."

"It's a ranch. A flip job just off Highway 93 at the base of North Table Mountain."

Abigail was quite sure that the look on her face demonstrated her surprise. "Did you flip it?"

"Am flipping it," he said as he took a sip from his wine. "The bedroom is gorgeous. The bathroom is to die for. That's where I started. I don't have much done in the kitchen. A sink and a microwave. The flooring is next, and then I can look at putting appliances back in. As for the living room, I have a futon and a card table."

Abigail sat back and pressed her hand to her chest as she laughed even harder. "I didn't see that coming. Will you take me someday, show me?"

"Absolutely. From the outside, which I had painted, and a nice front door added, you'd never know the inside is a mess. You do promise not to laugh at my housekeeping skills, correct?"

"I assume your housekeeping skills are fine and it's the house that's the problem. I know when I was painting this one, everything was in disarray."

Carson nodded. "Exactly." He held his glass again to toast. "Here's to making the old new again."

He tapped his glass to hers and then sipped. Abigail felt his words sucker punch her in the gut. That's exactly what he was doing, wasn't it? Taking what was run down and, making it new. She sipped her wine. Perhaps, she'd try to understand.

CHAPTER 18

*C*arson had nearly scraped everything off his dinner plate. Had it been that long since he'd had a home-cooked meal? His mother, though competent in the kitchen, was no gourmet. She had two or three good meals in her, but Abigail was a genius.

She laughed a genuine, and beautiful laugh when he told her so.

Abigail lifted her wine to her lips and took a sip. "You have no idea how I fretted over this dinner. Clare gave me the instructions. I'm good with instructions."

"Well, I could eat like this the rest of my life."

He saw her eyes widen before she sipped her wine again. Perhaps that scared her, but for some reason, it didn't scare him.

Carson sat back in his chair and sipped his wine. He studied her as she mixed the dressing around her leaves of lettuce, without taking a bite. "You don't like salad?"

"I eat too much of it at work."

Carson leaned his arms on the table. "Perhaps we should start having lunch together too. I'd hate to see you wither away like an uneaten salad."

"I promise you I'll never wither away. I enjoy food way too much."

"Well, whatever you eat looks good on you and so does that yellow dress. A ray of sunshine on a crisp fall day."

She watched him over the rim of her glass and sipped. "You're very good at this flirting. Should I worry about that?"

He sat back again and grinned widely. "Honestly, if I were any good at it I would assume I'd have been swept away by now." He reached across the table and gripped her hand. "Or maybe, I've just been waiting for the right girl to use my charm on."

Abigail set her wine down and pressed her free hand to her chest. "Wow. The right girl?"

"That scares you, doesn't it?"

Her eyes fixed on his, and her expression changed to a serious one. She shook her head. "No. It doesn't scare me at all."

SHE WATCHED THE HEAT FLICKER IN HIS EYES AS HE STOOD FROM the table and moved swiftly to her. He took her hand and brought her to her feet, pressing her against him.

Carson released her hair from the band that held it back and ran his fingers through it until it cascaded over her shoulders. Then, with his hand tangled in her blonde curls, he brought his mouth to hers with a passion she'd never felt before.

Abigail found herself gripping tightly to the front of his shirt just to hold herself up. She fought for breath because she searched for more—more passion—more heat.

Carson's hand moved down her back and gripped her bottom, pulling her even closer to him. This was the moment. There was no turning back. She was tumbling straight into love with the man who had her whole body ablaze with feelings and sensations. No images swirled in her head, no premonitions of what was to happen beyond this moment. His effect on her was different than any other person in the entire world. He was a blessing to her, in many ways.

He pressed his forehead to hers, and they both gasped. "Do we continue?" he asked with a ragged breath.

She couldn't vocalize her need. Instead, she nodded.

"Good," he said as he took possession of her mouth again, lifted her off the ground, and carried her to the sofa where he lowered her down without releasing the kiss.

Abigail's skirt rose up as Carson moved against her. His hands came to her breasts and caressed. His mouth worked against her throat. She reached between them and fumbled with the buttons on his shirt, until he sat up and released the buttons for himself, pulling the shirt from his body.

The need to touch his bare skin had her placing her hands on his chest. The fact that her hands were splayed on his skin and only electricity buzzed between them, made her want to love him more.

Carson managed the top of her dress down over her shoulders and arms, and flipped the hook on the front of her bra, exposing her to him. She heard the throaty groan that escaped him as he lowered his mouth to her breasts.

Abigail moved beneath him, the sensations overwhelming her as his mouth moved back to hers.

"I think this would be better if we moved," he said breathlessly as he took her mouth again. "Can I take you to your bed?"

Abigail gazed back at him. She'd never had a man in her bedroom, and wouldn't it be special for the first man that walked through the door to be the man she was going to marry?

"Yes," she sighed the word as he scooped her up and carried her down the hall.

IN THE DARKNESS OF A MOONLESS NIGHT, ABIGAIL'S HEAD RESTED

on Carson's bare chest. She heard his heartbeat, now in sync with hers. The experience had been more beautiful than she could've imagined.

What she thought might have started out as reckless, passionate sex, had carried into the bedroom as an evening of lovemaking. Carson was very attentive to her every need. There was no quick roll on the bed. Touches, kisses, and caresses lasted through the night. Now, he rested softly beneath her.

Her hand touched his bare skin, and all she felt was his heartbeat. It was an unbelievable moment, not worrying about seeing beyond the now. So, she might know that at some point this man would become her husband, but she was delighted in the fact that not everything would come to her by touching him.

Abigail let her eyes drift closed. This man would spend the first, what she figured would be many nights in her bed and her arms. She already loved him. There was no way she would tell him. She still didn't agree with everything he stood for. But she knew deep in her heart that she loved him.

CARSON'S ARMS HAD NEARLY GONE NUMB WITH ABIGAIL IN THEM. But he wouldn't move. He wasn't sure he ever wanted to move.

How is it possible that he happened into the store where this angel waited for him? He smiled as he thought about Mrs. Winters' absolution that they changed plans and go for tea. From that very moment he first watched her, his mind had been obsessively occupied by her. Was it possible to fall in love with somebody so quickly? Of course it was. Mrs. Winters had proved that, hadn't she?

He'd awakened from a deep sleep to see that she was still nestled up next to him. And now he lay there, in the silence of the night, just watching her.

She stirred. He saw the movement of her eyes beneath her eyelids, and her breathing began to grow heavier. She moved from his body, and then sat up and coughed. Again she coughed and sucked in a breath reaching for her throat.

"Abigail? Are you okay?" He asked frantically as he sat up and touched her. Her eyes were closed, and she coughed as though something was choking her.

Carson reached out to her and shook her. "Abigail, wake up!"

Her eyes flew open, and she continued to gasp for air. "Fire! Fire! Smoke is thick. We have to help."

Carson reached for her, but she climbed from the bed and quickly began to fumble through her drawers for something to wear.

He'd never seen anybody sleepwalk like this. It was quite scary.

"Abigail, you need to wake up."

She turned to him, obviously fully aware of what was going on. "Mrs. Winters. Her house is on fire."

He shook his head. "You're dreaming. Everybody's fine."

Abigail continued to get dressed. "You need to trust me. We need to go right now."

CHAPTER 19

*A*bigail dressed and started for the kitchen to grab her keys for her car before Carson had realized she was leaving with or without him. It was the strangest behavior he'd ever seen from her, or anyone else he'd ever known.

He ran back to the bedroom, pulled on his clothes, and ran out of the house as she started her car.

"Abigail, you're scaring the hell out of me," he hollered as he barely got the door shut before she backed out of the driveway.

Quickly, he snapped his seatbelt and held on.

He watched her face as she madly drove through the quiet streets of Golden toward the highway. If he'd ever seen the eyes of a madwoman, this was it.

"Slow down. You're going to kill someone," he demanded.

"If we don't get there, it will kill someone. You have to trust me."

"I would trust you if you told me what the hell is going on."

He watched her nearly strangle the steering wheel with her hands. "I saw it in a dream. If I see it in a dream, you have to believe."

So nothing in his life changed, he decided. He always could fall in love with the crazy ones.

Once Abigail had made it onto the highway, she sped toward the Genesee exit. Carson was sure he had signed a death sentence by getting into the car.

As the car turned up the winding road, he saw the flicker in the kitchen window. Mrs. Winters' house was on fire.

"Holy shit!" he yelled as Abigail slammed on the brakes and threw the car in park.

He pushed open his door and found he was running after Abigail as she headed toward the house.

Abigail ran up the front steps to the door. She tried the knob, but of course, it was locked. Frantically, she knocked on the door.

"Mrs. Winters! Mrs. Winters, are you in there?" she yelled.

"Back up," Carson instructed as he picked up a rock from her garden and threw it through the window of the front door. Taking off his coat, he wrapped it around his hand and broke the glass out. Reaching inside, he unlocked it and pushed it open.

The house was filled with smoke, and it burned his lungs as he moved in.

"Ellie. Ellie, can you hear me?"

He moved through the house toward the room where he knew she slept on the main floor. The smoke grew thicker, and he could feel the heat from the flames in the kitchen.

"I called 9-1-1," Abigail came up behind him and coughed.

"Get out of here. The smoke is toxic."

"She's in her bed. It's going to take both of us to get her out," Abigail said as she lifted her shirt over her nose.

It wasn't the time to ask, obviously she knew more than he could ever imagine. Carson kept a hand on the wall to guide him towards the bedroom. Luckily, her door was closed. He opened the door for him and Abigail, letting enough smoke in that Mrs. Winters stirred. Then he shut it again.

"Mrs. Winters, it's Carson. Wake up. There's a fire."

He saw Abigail moving to put a blanket at the door. "This window goes out to the side yard. We need to go out this window."

He gave her a nod in the dark and moved to Mrs. Winters. "Mrs. Winters, do you hear me?"

He could see her silhouette, she sat up and raised her hand to him. "Jeffery? You did come back," she said calmly. "You said there's a fire? Will you help me get out?"

Carson wasn't about to correct her. "Yes, Gran. It's me. My friend Abigail and I are going to take you out the window. We are not going to let you get hurt."

As he managed her from the bed, he stepped on her slippers.

"Gran, put on your slippers."

"That's a good idea, Jeffery." She slipped her feet into the slippers. "Abigail? You're the girl I share my birthday with, correct?"

"Yes, Mrs. Winters. Now, I have the window open. Jeffery is going to go outside and help you out."

"Okay," Mrs. Winters said as the three of them moved to the window.

Just as Carson swung his legs out of the window, a fire truck pulled up followed by an ambulance. He called to them to hurry to him.

"I have Ellie Winters here. Eighty-two-years-old, she's coming through the window." He turned back toward the women. "Gran, the firefighters are here to help you. Let them help you."

"Carson, you never call me Gran," she said clearly. "The two of you get out of here, and let the firefighters do their job."

Carson was helped out of the window by a firefighter, and then Abigail. Two more firefighters climbed in the window, and a few moments later, they brought Mrs. Winters out.

The paramedics brought a stretcher to the window and laid her on it just as the other firefighters got the water on the fire.

Carson and Abigail were pushed away from the house and toward the street as neighbors began to emerge. He kept his distance from her as he wrapped his head around what had happened.

Abigail had warned him about the fire. She'd awoken, choking on smoke, or at least seemed to have been. How in the hell could she have known the house was on fire? Had she planned it? She'd been in the house earlier that day.

His stomach knotted at the thought that she might have done something so devious. Then he remembered when he'd gone to the store earlier he'd wanted to ask her about the death of Katie Meadows.

Carson looked at Abigail who stood watching Mrs. Winters' house with tears in her eyes. Did someone who had it in them to harm someone cry when they stood back and watched the destruction unfold?

He didn't want to believe it, but how could he not? There were too many things that pointed to Abigail Weston, leaving him unsure about the woman he thought he was falling in love with.

Carson moved to her, and when he reached out and touched her arm, she jumped away from him as if he had burned her.

"Are you okay?" he asked, noticing the shock in her eyes.

"Yes," she said, quickly keeping her distance. "Her family is on their way to the hospital. You should go too. Take my car. I'll call Clare for a ride."

Abigail turned to walk away, and Carson reached for her arm and spun her back to him. Again, she pulled from him as though it hurt. "What is wrong with you?"

"You need to go."

"I'm not leaving you here."

"Then I'll take you back to my place," she said as she watched the police and the firefighters discuss the fire and then look toward them. "Let's go."

Abigail walked straight to her car and Carson followed, but she stopped as a police officer approached her.

"Ms. Weston?"

"Yes," she said, and he heard her voice waver.

The officer looked up at him. "Mr. Stone?"

"Yes," Carson answered, keeping an eye on Abigail's expression as she fought back tears.

"I have a few questions for you if you don't mind. Then you're free to go. I'm sure you want to head to the hospital with Mrs. Winters."

Carson nodded. "We would like to do that."

"Were you here when the fire started?"

Afraid of what Abigail might say, Carson stepped up to stand next to her. He looked at the officer. "No. We both visited this morning, and Mrs. Winters wasn't thinking quite straight. She's in the early stages of Alzheimer's."

The officer made a note of that. "What made you come back?"

"We thought we should check on her."

"At three in the morning?"

"Yes," Carson answered quickly, knowing it would sound more convincing if there were no thinking about it. "I try to keep an eye on her. Her family just learned of her diagnosis, so they haven't been able to make care plans for her yet."

The officer tucked his notebook back in his pocket. "Ms. Weston, are you doing okay? Perhaps you should get checked out since you were in the house."

"I will. Thank you," Abigail said.

"It was lucky that you two happened by. They didn't see anything physically wrong with Mrs. Winters, but they will check her out thoroughly."

Carson held his hand out to shake the officer's hand. "Thank you."

As he walked away, Abigail climbed into her car and sat behind the wheel. She didn't start the engine when Carson sat in the passenger seat.

He waited a moment before he spoke. "Can you drive, or would you like me to drive?"

"You don't trust me," she said staring out the front window, the key gripped between her fingers. "You think I'm crazy. You think I'd harm people for my own joy. This evening you thought you were in love with me, but now you're questioning that."

If Carson spoke, he was sure he'd choke on his own words. Was she a mind reader?

"Head back to your house. Let's talk."

"Don't you want to go to the hospital?" She finally looked up at him.

"Does she need me to?" he asked, assuming she'd answer as if she knew the answer.

Abigail shook her head. "She's fine. She thinks that Jeffery pulled her from her bed and walked her out the front door."

He didn't say another word as she started the engine and drove down the mountain back to her house. He'd take the quiet drive to try and piece together the questions he was going to have, and he hoped that she'd answer them truthfully. If she didn't, he was going to have one strong dose of heartbreak.

CHAPTER 20

*A*bigail busied herself making coffee as Carson called Mrs. Winters' family for an update.

When he tucked away his phone, Abigail set a cup of coffee in front of him.

"Is she doing okay?"

Carson thought for a moment before he answered, wondering if she already knew the answer. "She's physically fine. She doesn't remember the fire, just the conversation with Jeffery, and you."

"Odd, isn't it? Why would she remember me if she doesn't remember you?"

Carson ran his finger over the rim of the mug as Abigail sat down at the table across from him. He watched her purposely avoid eye contact with him. "She associates me with Jeffery. I think that's why we've always been so close. I took his place."

"And I'm new."

"You're a kindred soul. You share the same birthday."

That made her smile behind her mug as she'd lifted it and took a sip. But when she lowered it, her demeanor changed.

"Go ahead," she said. "I'm used to the questions."

Curious, he leaned in with his arms on the table. "What questions?"

"How did I know she was sick? How did I know about the fire? Those are only the first questions on your list. I'm surprised you're sitting here at all." She stood and walked to the counter. Taking the rag from the sink, she began to clean where there was no mess. A moment later she threw the rag in the sink and turned to him, her hands gripping the counter. "Ask about her, Carson. Just ask."

Cautiously, he rose and moved to her. "Her?"

"It's been eating at you all day. You want to know if I killed Katie Meadows."

Maybe she was a mind reader. Carson tucked his hands into his pockets because he could suddenly begin to feel them shake.

"How did you know I was going to ask you about that? I didn't tell anyone about her."

"You told me," she said sniffing back tears. "You don't know you told me, but you did."

"Abigail, you're starting to scare me. What's going on?"

Pushing the fallen wisps of hair from her face, Abigail sat back down at the table, but Carson stayed where he was. Part of him wanted to run out the back door and never look back, but his heart said to stay.

ABIGAIL SAT QUIETLY AT THE TABLE TWISTING A NAPKIN AROUND her fingers which she'd pulled from the holder. When she'd moved to Golden she'd hoped to never tell this story again, but here she was, another person staring at her as if she'd done wrong. Where would she run after Carson left her house and never spoke to her again? When the police came back later to question her about the fire at Mrs. Winters' house, what would she tell them? How would her life change without Carson in it?

He was patient. She knew that much. She wasn't sure how

long she'd sat there in silence, but he hadn't pushed or asked again. Now it was time to tell him her secret and wonder if he'd stay or run.

"Promise me one thing," she said as she looked up at him. "When you leave, go calmly. It takes the pain away a little bit."

"Because what you're about to tell me is going to make me want to leave?"

"In my experience, no one wants to stick around."

She watched as he considered, and his jaw tightened. "I think I'll make up my own damn mind where that's concerned."

She pushed the tangled napkin aside and sat her hands flat on the table. Taking a deep breath, she gathered the strength to tell him her secret.

"Katie Meadows was the sister of someone I knew. She was ten when she disappeared. I woke up one night, from a very vivid dream, and I knew where they would find her. And they did."

"A dream? You saw her in the river in a dream?"

"I see you've done your homework." She wasn't sure how she felt about that, but he had every right. "Yes, they found her in the river just as I said that they would. That was the biggest premonition I'd had to date. Others like knowing my grandmother had a tumor, for telling my mother not to drive a certain direction and then there was an accident, those were little in comparison."

Carson took a long drawn and breath. "Premonitions? Is that what you're telling me you had?"

"Yes."

He nodded and folded his arms in front of him. "You told me yesterday morning that there would be a fire. In the middle of the night, you woke in a fire. That was a premonition?"

"Yes. I see things in my dreams, but I also see them when I touch somebody. That's how I knew Mrs. Winters was sick. She told me."

"She told you?" His tone was as sarcastic as those from her past.

"The day I met you both, she touched my hand."

Carson moved to the table and rested his hands on the back of the chair. His knuckles went white, and she knew he was holding on for dear life. "You touched me. You've touched me everywhere," he reminded her. "What do you see from me?"

Abigail took another napkin from the holder and wrapped it around her fingers. "That's the very strange part." She looked up at him. "I don't see anything."

He snorted a laugh then paced the kitchen raking his fingers through his hair. "So only old ladies?"

"No," she said as she stood, feeling as though now she needed to defend herself. "You're one of the first people I've never seen anything with. Except for one time and..."

"One time?" He dropped his hands to his hips and held them still there. "What did you see?"

"It was the day I asked you to come to the shop and get the pastries. I had seen you getting hurt. Someone who was against your building proposal, they wanted to hurt you."

Abigail watched the anger diminish, and his skin began to grow pale. "I had a threat on my voicemail. Someone said something about the church being sacred and my car was not. I remember thinking they were going to do something to my car, perhaps I'd seen too many movies, and I thought that there was a bomb under it."

"I couldn't tell you exactly what I saw, except that you were hurt, and yes, it had something to do with your car. I knew that if I got you out of there before you would've left normally, maybe you would've been safe."

Carson pulled back the chair and sat down. "That's how you knew Mrs. Winters had Alzheimer's. Before we knew."

"Yes."

"And you must've seen something that day you met my mother. Something happened, and you could barely stand on your feet."

Abigail took a cleansing breath. "It's not a gift, Carson. It's some kind of curse. I don't want to know these things. The glory is when I do touch you I don't see anything. I get to enjoy the moment with you. I do want to enjoy the moments with you. No matter what I've seen." Once she said it, she saw his head rise, and she wished she could take that back.

Carson stood and gripped her shoulders. "If there is something bad, you need to tell me. If something is going to happen to me, or my family, or you…"

"Nothing bad happens."

"Damnit, tell me."

"This is where everything is ruined."

"What the hell does that mean?"

"The moment I touched Mrs. Winters hand, I saw you and me."

"Hooking up?"

She pushed away from his grip. "Is that what this all was? Just a hook up to you?"

"No. I thought it was so much more."

"And with all I know, the moment is lost. There is no mystique. It seems like a chore now."

"And if it involves me, you'd better damn well tell me."

She stepped to him, angrily. "Fine. What I saw was you and me. Husband and wife. When I went back the other day, to see if anything had changed, I saw more. Not only did I see that fire that was coming, I saw us. I saw our wedding. I saw our house. And I saw our children. As much as I want all of that, it would be nice not to have it sprawled out in front of me like a story I can read."

When she finished, she looked up at him and noticed his eyes were wide. "I felt all of that last night." He ran his hand over his stubbled chin. "I decided last night that I knew I wanted you. I wanted to get married. And of course, have children."

"Great. Maybe we can skip everything else and just start today."

Carson reached her hands, squeezed them both gently. "And you told other people things like this? Finding Katie and other things and they didn't believe you."

"No. Most of the town still thinks I killed her. But there was no proof. Because I didn't do it. And I saw that police officer's eyes last night. Why would you and I be driving around at 3 AM with nothing else to do? I didn't put Mrs. Winters in harm's way. In fact, I tried to get you to get her out of the house."

"Maybe had you told me this when you came to my office..."

"You could have had time to run like hell," she countered.

Carson went silent. "Maybe you're right."

CHAPTER 21

*A*bigail sat in her screened in porch, and she hated that she did. A quilt her grandmother had made her was wrapped around her legs. She had been nursing the same cup of the tea for an hour, and it was bitter cold.

Carson had decided to leave, and she didn't blame him. What kind of lunatic tells you she knows the future? What man ever wants to hear who he's going to marry, how he's going to marry, and how many children he will have? Not to mention that she sounded crazy telling him how she knew of Mrs. Winters' illness, and the fire.

What she had to remember, was that they had saved her life. They got there before she could have walked out to the hallway when the house was engulfed.

Later, when the chaos around her settled a bit, Abigail would go to Mrs. Winters. Why had she been the one to give her so much information? Carson said because they were kindred souls, the shared birthday. But she didn't know if that was true. Plenty of people were born on October fourteenth. If it was, in fact, a day of the sixth sense, wouldn't the world know about that?

Sunday was a day of peace and quiet for her, but in her head,

119

it was anything but quiet. She missed him already, and she hated that she did. It shouldn't matter that he walked out the door. There was no reason for him to come back through it either.

News of the fire had gotten to Clare. She had called and wanted to know what she could do. There was nothing to do, Abigail told her. Mrs. Winters was in the hospital, and Abigail was sitting alone wallowing in self-pity. It shouldn't have been surprised her that Clare drove over with a crockpot full of soup. At least it made Abigail laugh. Only Clare would always have a crockpot of soup ready to go. Then again, so had their grandmother.

As she sat at her kitchen table, still in her pajamas at three o'clock in the afternoon, Clare handed her a bowl of soup.

Clare sat down across from her with her bowl. "Grandma said there were always reasons for soup."

Abigail laughed. "I sometimes wonder if she'd still be around if they'd they found that tumor."

"Well, I can guarantee you if you ever tell a family member they have a tumor, they'll listen."

"Fantastic. I'd rather not know. Look what good it's done for me." She lifted her soup to her lips, blew, and slurped. "I decided I either need to shut myself up in my house forever and never talk to anyone again, or open some ten dollar psychic reading stand."

"We can set you up a table at the tea shop," Clare joked, and it lightened the mood.

"It wouldn't work for every person. I didn't see things when I touched Carson. Not even when we…"

She noticed her cousin stopping mid-spoonful. Her eyes wide open.

"Don't act like you didn't know that was coming. I told you I was going to marry him, right?"

Clare took a napkin from the holder on the table and wiped her mouth. "You did. I didn't think you liked him. He's going to tear down that church."

"I suppose now I can focus my efforts on that. Maybe if he saw me at the meeting coming up, he'd walk out. Leave the whole project and go," she said with her hands in the air in a grand gesture. "Who knows, I might just save the town."

"So you're not going to marry him?"

Abigail pushed back her soup and rested her arms on the table. "I doubt it. I wouldn't want a lunatic for a spouse."

"Does it work that way? Can you change fate?"

"I don't know. Later, I'm going to visit Mrs. Winters. Maybe she can tell me."

Clare held up her spoon, using it to gesture towards Abigail. "You think she knows something. More than just transferring the premonition to you. You think she understands it."

Abigail shrugged. "I have nothing to lose, right? Besides, there was a moment in her bedroom when we were getting her out of the fire. She kept talking to Jeffery, her grandson and Carson's best friend. He's been dead for sixteen years or more. Carson thought she was confusing him with Jeffery. But I think she was talking to Jeffery."

"As if he was there in the room with you guys?"

"Something like that. Anyway, it was contact with her that made me see Carson. I just want to know what happens now."

CARSON DECIDED THAT SUNDAY MORNING WAS THE PERFECT TIME to start the flooring in the kitchen.

He took the old beat up pickup truck, which he used for renovation, and spent the morning at the Home Depot. He wanted to go to Mrs. Winters, but he opted to call her son instead. After having her call him Jeffery, he didn't want to confuse her any further.

Her son had confirmed that she was fine. But they had decided to get her some assistance. The house would be uninhabitable for a while, and at least she wasn't arguing about not getting to go home.

The tile in the kitchen would take him days. Mostly because he wasn't very good at it, and because of his impatience he'd already cracked two of them. But, it would keep his mind off Abigail.

He couldn't decide how he felt about what she had told him. Part of him wanted to call her crazy and have her locked up. The other part of him wanted to kiss away any pain she may have.

If everything she had said was true, he had decided that was a terrible way to live. She had a gift that could help other people, but most of them, like him, were skeptical. How badly had she been treated back home to make her move this far away? He didn't believe that she had killed Katie Meadows. He might have for a few days, or had hoped she hadn't. But now, he truly didn't believe she did. But how many people back home still thought she had?

And now, what would come after the fire and Mrs. Winters' house? Surely once a fire investigator was in there, they would know that Abigail was innocent.

God, he hoped that's what they would find.

Later, much later, he would go back to her and apologize. He hadn't stormed out, as she asked him not to. He hadn't said much either. There was too much to sort out in his head.

As he lined up the tiles and inserted the spacers, he thought about the church on Ford Street. If they'd had a prior argument, it was about that church. Why was it so important to her that it didn't get torn down?

He'd love to keep the integrity of the building. However, it needed to be gutted. The structure was unsafe. There were a few things he could probably do to keep some of the church, which they hadn't figured into the designs, but—he dropped another tile and it shattered.

"Shit!" He sat back on his heels and looked at the mess around him. This wasn't clearing his mind as he had hoped it would. He needed a good long walk. The mess could wait.

Carson walked back to his bedroom and pulled out his running shoes. He'd take a walk to the top of the stairs at Mother Cabrini's shrine. The view always inspired him and cleared his head. Perhaps a brisk cold walk to the top would do just that.

CHAPTER 22

*T*here was something about hospitals that made Abigail sick to her stomach. She kept her hands in tight fists, in the pockets of her coat. She was afraid to touch anything. These walls could talk, and she was sure they would talk to her.

When she had reached the room where Mrs. Winters was, she stood outside for a moment. Perhaps it was a mistake to see her. The woman couldn't remember who Carson was, and he was an important part of her life.

"Abigail." She heard her name called from the room. "Please come in here."

Abigail closed her eyes and let out a long steady breath. It was Mrs. Winters' voice which called to her.

Abigail moved to the door, which was luckily open just the slightest bit, and pushed it open with her arm.

Mrs. Winters sat in her bed, her eyes bright, and her smile warm. Abigail hadn't been sure what she would see, but she was sure that Mrs. Winters wasn't going to look as fantastic as she did.

"You look good," Abigail said, her voice cracking a bit.

"I am good. Thanks to you and Carson, I'm perfect."

Abigail completely believed her. Had they told her of her illness? Perhaps it was better if she didn't know.

"I'm glad you doing well. I wanted to stop by and make sure."

Mrs. Winters narrowed her eyes at Abigail. "You and Carson have had an argument. Over me?"

How was she supposed to answer that? It wasn't directly over Mrs. Winters.

"A misunderstanding, perhaps."

Mrs. Winters clasped her hands together on her lap. "Abigail, darling, hold no secrets with me. We are alike. Born on the same day. I've seen your life, darling. It's a beautiful life."

Tears immediately choked Abigail, and she coughed trying to clear her throat. But the tears came. "How do you see it?"

"The same way you do. The moment I touched your hand, I saw everything, and so did you. He's your soulmate, Abigail. And he's a good one."

Abigail wiped away the tears that streamed down her cheeks. She'd never had anyone in her life who truly understood what she was going through. Mrs. Winters understood her completely. "I've always felt so alone. People don't understand."

"Some of us do. Why do you think I married my husband so quickly? I knew he was the right one. It was more than seeing it in my dreams, or when I touched him. I knew it in my heart."

"But I don't see anything when I touch him. Not when I kiss him or make love to him," she said as she felt the heat rising her cheeks.

The smile widened on Mrs. Winters dry lips. "No need to be embarrassed around me, darling." She reached for Abigail's hand, and without thinking, Abigail took hers.

She saw Carson, standing atop a mountain. She saw him come to her with flowers. Instinctively, she pulled back from Mrs. Winters.

"I'm sorry. I'm afraid to see anymore."

"You shouldn't be, but I understand." Mrs. Winters rested her head against the pillow. "My time here is almost over. They don't want me to know that. But it is."

Abigail wiped her cheeks again and willed herself to stop crying. "You have a little time left."

"You and I know that, but still not very long. It is long enough for me to have tea with my birthday girl."

"Absolutely. I'll bring the tea party to you if I have to."

"You won't have to." Mrs. Winters took a moment, and Abigail assumed she had more to say. "I'm not crazy, you know. I knew it was you and Carson helping me out of my bedroom that night, but Jeffery was there too."

Abigail nodded. "I knew that. I didn't sense or see him," she clarified. "But I knew that you did."

"He's preparing me. When the time is right, he'll be waiting for me."

Abigail wondered how that could make anyone calm. But for Mrs. Winters, it seemed to.

"I should let you get some rest."

"Abigail, don't let him go. He loves you. He'll do anything for you. But be careful, in doing so there is danger. I can't see it, but I can see beyond it— sometimes." She lifted her hands in a gesture. "Take care of each other. In your heart, you know this is true love."

Mrs. Winters closed her eyes, and Abigail took that as her signal to leave.

As she walked out to her car, she wondered what it had meant to see Carson atop a mountain. Was that literal? How was she to find him on top of a mountain? Well, he was the one that walked out or was pushed out. Abigail would wait for him to come to her.

Just as Abigail moved to the front door to turn the sign to

closed, on Monday afternoon, she saw Carson leaning against his car, a bouquet of flowers in his arms. He wasn't moving toward the store. Obviously, he was waiting for her to notice him.

Abigail opened the door, locking it behind her, and sliding the keys into her apron pocket. The October air had grown cold, and she crossed her arms in front of her to keep her warm.

"I was hoping you would look up," he said as she walked toward him.

"You could have come in."

"I wasn't so sure." He handed her the flowers. "I don't think there's another woman I've ever given this many flowers to. I've missed you."

Abigail lifted her eyes from the flowers to him. "I've missed you too."

"Mrs. Winters said you went to see her."

"I did," she said as her voice quivered from the cold.

Carson opened his car door and retrieved his coat from inside. He moved to her and placed it over her shoulders.

"Thank you."

He nodded. "I owe you an apology. I just didn't know how to wrap my head around what you told me. I've been set straight. I'm sorry."

Abigail thought on that for a moment. "I assume this has to do with a conversation you had with Mrs. Winters?"

"Trust me. I'm not one to argue with her."

"Are you claiming to understand me, just to satisfy her?"

Carson reached for Abigail's hand and pressed a kiss to her fingers. "No. I'm willing to understand because I love you."

Abigail felt her lips tremble. "Carson…"

He pressed a finger to her lips. "Don't, don't say anything. I don't understand this gift, or curse, that you have. But I under-stand now that you're not the only person. I hope that through your gift, you see good things, and want to keep me around."

In her heart, she had been waiting for this moment. She

hadn't wanted to keep him, in the beginning. He stood for things she didn't believe in. If she didn't take a chance, she would regret it forever. She knew that she loved him, Mrs. Winters was right.

"I don't want to lose you."

"I'm not going anywhere. Let me help you finish up. I want to show you my home now. We'll pick up some takeout on the way."

CHAPTER 23

They had stopped for Chinese food. Abigail sat in his luxury car with the bag on her lap. Carson drove just north of town, and through a neighborhood Abigail was familiar with.

"Clare lives just around the corner," she said. "I remember this house being for sale."

"Then you remember what a mess it was," he said as he drove into the gravel that was used as a driveway.

From the looks of the outside, she wasn't sure there had been any improvement. Then again, he had told her that much. She would save any judgment until she saw the inside.

Carson turned off the engine and opened his door. "Don't move." He skirted the front of the car, and came to her door and opened it. "I'll take this," he said as he took the bag from her. "I know where all the divots in the floor are. I don't want you to fall."

Abigail laughed as she climbed from the car. "If this is a dangerous place to be, why would I want to be here?"

"Because I'm here," he said with a wink, and then took her hand, and led her to the house.

Carson unlocked the door and pushed it in. He reached around the wall and turned on the light. Abigail held her breath and realized that the disappointment was real.

"I told you, this will be the last room to get done. No judging. Wait until you see the bathroom and my bedroom. Oh, and the kitchen floor."

Abigail plastered a smile on her face. "I'll keep an open mind."

Carson closed and locked the front door. He took her hand and led her through to the kitchen. Again, he turned on the light.

"I was trying to get the floor finished yesterday. But my mind wasn't clear enough. So I took a walk to the top of Mother Cabrini's shine."

Carson turned to her when she gasped. "Top of the mountain."

"What does that mean?"

She considered for a moment before going forward with the conversation. It was okay to tell him. He promised to try to understand.

"Mrs. Winters took my hand, and I saw you on top of the mountain."

Carson gave her hand to squeeze. "I guess you'll never have to track my phone then will you?"

She laughed, as the moment intended humor. But she worried, as Carson held her hand and she saw nothing.

Carson, still carrying the bag of food, led her down the hallway and to the back of the house. He pushed open another door, this time she was impressed.

"Oh, this is beautiful."

Abigail leaned in through the doorway, afraid to walk into the room. The dark plush carpet, accented by earthy brown walls made the space cozy and warm. The trim, painted white, gave it the perfect contrast. He had an enormous king size bed, which was made perfectly with a duvet and accent pillows. She couldn't help but wonder if he planned to bring her there. An entertainment center was built into the wall adjacent the bed. Who needed a television that big in their bedroom.

"You can come in," he said as he walked into the room. "I have a table where we can eat." He pointed to a little table in the corner.

"I don't want to walk through here with my shoes on."

"Considering the construction mess and the rest of the house, I highly recommend you do leave them on."

Abigail stepped into the bedroom. "You eat in here?"

"You did see my kitchen, right?"

"So you're basically living in your bedroom?"

Carson set the bag on the small table and looked around the room.

"Yep. But not forever. C'mon, sit down."

Abigail walked to the table and sat in one of the chairs. "You have two chairs."

"And you're afraid I bring other people in here to eat?"

She shrugged. Yes, unfortunately, that was exactly what she was thinking.

Carson began to take out the containers and set them on the table. "It's a table for the patio when I get the deck redone. It came with two chairs. My kitchen table is in storage, and this keeps it out of the way. Hence two chairs at my table in my bedroom."

Abigail let her shoulders drop. "I'm sorry. I don't have any right to cast my judgment on you."

"Sure you do. We're sleeping together."

"We slept together."

"And I have all intentions to keep doing so," he continued as he opened the containers, and handed her a pair of chopsticks. "This isn't a fling. It's not something laid out like a roadmap either. I know what you say you saw, but every day we make decisions that change the course we are on. So that's how I choose to see all of this."

Abigail picked up a container and stirred the noodles around with the chopsticks. "Mrs. Winters said because she saw her husband and the path before them, that's why she married him so quickly."

Carson slurped up a noodle from his container as he watched her from over the top of it. "You think we should get married?"

"No. I just want you to know you're not locked into anything. Just because I say I saw it, and Mrs. Winters saw it too, doesn't mean you have to believe it or rush it."

"Then we'll take our time."

Abigail set the container down and crossed her arms in front of her. "She was talking to Jeffery the other night when we were taking her out of her house."

That had him stopping his acquisition of the perfect bite and setting his container on the table. "She was talking to him? She didn't just think I was him?"

She shook her head. "She said he's coming for her, and when she's ready, she'll go with him. Admittedly, she knows it sounds crazy, and that's probably why she only told me about it. Carson, she's not afraid."

"I am."

"Me too."

He reached across the table and took her hand. "Do you see anything when I hold your hand?"

Abigail shook her head. "Nothing."

"And you think this is all some curse?"

"Wouldn't you?"

"Of course I would. I don't want to know everything. Okay, maybe lottery numbers."

"It doesn't work that way."

He lifted her hand to his lips and pressed a kiss to her fingers. "Go with me tomorrow to see Mrs. Winters. She seems to embrace her gift. I want to understand it from that side."

Tears welled in Abigail's eyes. "You're willing to accept all of this? I'm living it, and I think I sound crazy."

"You already know I love you. Even if I didn't say the words, you already knew. Love means I take time to understand what's going on in your life. What has always gone on. It's more than just the hairs on the back of your neck standing up when you sense a spider, Abi. It's like a horrific gift. I want to understand it."

Abigail sniffed back the tears. "Oh, Carson, I think you already do."

CHAPTER 24

*C*arson knew better than to go to the hospital to see Mrs. Winters without taking her a bouquet of roses, so he'd stopped on their way there. Her son had called and said she was in high spirits and ready to leave. They were holding her for one more day, just until they were sure she could go to the new facility where she'd live.

Hearing that made Carson's heart ache. He knew that the health of some seniors declined when they were put into housing facilities, and it worried him that Mrs. Winters would give up on life. Though, he couldn't imagine her doing so. He'd never known anyone who embraced every part of life—the good and the bad.

But, Abigail had said her time was almost up. She'd even said Mrs. Winters knew that too. Why wasn't he ready for it?

Abigail reached for his hand as they sat in the car out in front of the hospital. He realized when she reached for his hand that he'd sat there too long thinking about what waited for them when they went in, and what waited for Mrs. Winters when she got out.

"Are you going to be okay?" Abigail asked as she gave his hand a gentle squeeze.

"When Jeffery died, his grandmother was my strength. She had her own kids to worry about, and the grief over her grandson. But she made sure I was okay. Over the past few years, we've grown very close. It's hard to know she won't be going home."

Silence returned between them. Carson wondered if there would be calm for him when he saw Mrs. Winters. Would Jeffery be there? It was true, right? He believed Abigail and in her ability. Still sounded crazy in his head.

Carson finally opened the car door, and Abigail followed suit. Hand in hand they walked into the hospital. They remained silent as they rode the elevator to the third floor, and walked to Mrs. Winters room.

Glenn Winters, Jeffery's father, sat next to his mother's bed. They both had their attention directed toward the television. The movie they were watching was in black-and-white, a favorite pastime of Mrs. Winters.

Glenn saw them at the door first and stood.

"Carson," he said as he walked across the room shook his hand. "I was hoping I'd get to see you soon. I wanted to thank you for getting Mom out of that house. I'm eternally grateful to you."

Carson felt the sting of his words in his chest. He wished they could have said the same thing to him years ago when Jeffery died. Though they never blamed him, Carson always felt guilty.

"Glenn, this is Abigail Weston."

Glenn didn't reach his hand out to shake hers. Instead, he pulled her in and hugged her tightly. "Mom has told me all about you. Thank you for going to her."

He watched as the tears filled Abigail's eyes when he stepped back.

Abigail wiped her cheeks. "I'm glad we got there in time."

Glenn turned back to his mother. "I'm going to go get something to eat. I'll bring you back something," he promised.

As he walked out of the room, he patted Carson on the shoulder.

Carson moved to the bedside, and leaned in and kissed Mrs. Winters on the cheek. "How are you feeling?"

"Cooped up. I'm ready to fly."

Carson chuckled. "I'll bet you are. Can Abigail and I sit with you for a bit?"

"Of course you can. Abigail, I'm very happy to see you."

Abigail moved to her, kissed her on the cheek just as Carson had before. "I'm glad you're doing so well."

He noticed that the kiss was quick, and she didn't touch her. Was she afraid of what she might see?

Abigail sat in the chair next to the bed, and Carson took the chair on the other side. He wasn't even sure where to begin, but he needed a few answers for himself.

He reached for Mrs. Winters' hand, and she smiled sweetly at him. "Ask your questions, sweetheart. You want to. You're confused."

Carson noticed the smile that crept across Abigail's lips. He took a deep breath and thought about what he wanted to know.

"I'm not sure where to begin," he said. "This is quite new to me. I've never given much thought to abilities like this. And I didn't know you had them."

Mrs. Winters laughed. "Most people are close-minded. It's not something you talk about a lot."

"So that day we met Abigail," he began as he shifted a glance towards her, "you knew everything about her. Didn't you?"

"Oh, sweetheart, why do you think I wanted to go there?"

Carson sat back and chuckled. "You've always amazed me."

"And you me," Mrs. Winters replied. "It's not easy, Carson. I'm sure Abigail has shared that with you." She gave Abigail a kind smile, before turning her attention back to him. "Her gift is not getting a reading from you. My poor husband, he couldn't take a potato chip without me knowing. It was probably a curse for him as well."

"It saved your life. All that matters," he admitted.

Mrs. Winters shrugged as folding her hands over her stomach. "I'm glad you kids were there. I've never seen my demise in a fire. Just so you know, I'll just continue sleeping."

Carson fisted his hands to keep them from shaking. He didn't want to know how she would die, or when.

"Abigail told me you talk to Jeffery."

The smile returned to Mrs. Winters dry lips. "Oh, yes, honey. He's comforted me for years. Of course, I would rather have had him here with me all this time, but he has been waiting on the other side."

"And that's why you don't talk about it, right? It does sound crazy."

Mrs. Winters shrugged. "I'm much too old to care who thinks I'm crazy, Carson. But yes, that's why no one talks about it. And I knew his death traumatized you. You've never quite recovered. Abigail is here now, explore the future."

Carson glanced toward Abigail, who sat very quietly in the chair. "I'm sorry I walked out. You need my support, emotionally. I'm sorry I ever even considered you had anything to do with Katie Meadows' death. Obviously, I'm not open-minded enough."

He watched as Abigail brushed another tear from her cheek. "I'm not sure I am either," she admitted. "Until I met Mrs. Winters, I'd never known anyone else with such a gift. I don't want to see what will happen. I want to experience it."

He reached his hand across the bed to take hers. "We'll experience it together," he promised.

Mrs. Winters began to laugh. "Oh children, you make me very happy. Remember that the name Ellie is a great name for a little girl."

Abigail pulled her hand back quickly as if Mrs. Winters had given her some deep information. Carson knew to laugh. The old woman's sense of humor was something you had to get used to.

When Glenn reappeared at the door, he looked at his mother with a smile. "Good news, they're coming to spring you."

Mrs. Winters let out an exasperated sigh. "It's about damn time." She turned her head toward Abigail. "I'll be at your shop for our birthday. Carson said you'll join us, and I'm going to hold you to that."

Abigail had tucked her hands into the pockets of her jacket. "I look forward to that."

She turned to leave the room as Carson gave Mrs. Winters another kiss on the cheek. But she raised her hand to his cheek and held him near. She studied him closely. "Your plans for the church are perfect. She will understand. There's no need to change."

Carson processed the information for a moment. "Okay," he said, not truly understanding her comment. He had thought about redesigning it, but there had been no plans to go forward with it.

He shook Glenn's hand and promised Mrs. Winters he would be there to pick her up for their birthday tea.

Abigail waited just outside the room for him. He moved to her, placing his hands on her cheeks, and kissed her softly. "Thank you for coming. That woman is very special to me, and you are very special to her. I'm glad she saw us together."

Abigail rested her hands on his shoulders. "I'm glad too."

CHAPTER 25

*C*arson sat at his desk, as he had most of the week, looking at the blueprints for the Ford Street church project. He couldn't get Mrs. Winters' words out of his head. What had she meant to go ahead, and Abigail would understand?

They'd been living together for the past week, though not formally. They hadn't moved into one location, but they'd eaten dinner together and slept in the same bed each night. In the course of talking about work, they'd talked about his projects, but Abigail hadn't forced her opinion on him about the building at all. She listened, then steered the conversation to something else, but she didn't fight him or suggest anything to him.

Was Mrs. Winters trying to tell him that he should just keep working on the project, that Abigail had stopped caring?

He didn't believe that either.

But he'd wanted to change it, just a bit. Carson had been working on keeping the footprint of the church intact. He'd even had the architect working on it, but it was going to cost more, since the building was in bad shape.

He was concentrating so hard that he didn't notice anyone in his doorway until he heard them clear their throat.

Carson lifted his head to see Abigail standing there with her hip against the doorjamb and a bottle of wine in her hand.

"What are you doing?" Carson smiled as he leaned back in his chair.

"I came to see if you could leave early for the day. I just received this gift from my parents, along with a very nice picnic basket."

"What's the occasion?" He asked as she sauntered to his desk, and skirted around it to stand in front of him.

"Six month anniversary of the tea shop."

She stood in front of him, and he raised his hands to her hips. "Six months, huh? Amazing how successful you can be in half a year."

Abigail smiled. "I didn't know all of this would happen when I moved here. I guess deep down inside I knew that the store would be a success, but I had no idea it would bring me you."

Carson stood so that he could look her in the eye. "I'm so glad you came here with your dreams. Mrs. Winters would say it was fate."

"I think it was," she said as she lifted to her toes and kissed him gently. "Can you leave?"

Carson looked at the plans on his desk and thought about the proposal he needed to write up. "Sure. You don't celebrate successes like this every day. Let me clear off my desk."

Abigail turned around and looked down at the blueprints. "The church?"

"Yes."

He watched as she studied it. Did she know what she was looking at? Did it all make sense?

"There's a lot of planning that goes into this," she noted.

He waited for a comment, but she didn't say a word. "Where should we go to celebrate?" he asked, which had her turning back to him.

"My house has a living room and a couch where we could kick up our feet. We could even build a fire since it's a bit chilly out."

"That sounds nice," he agreed as he brushed his fingers through her hair. "Right now, just time with you would be perfect."

Carson pulled his hand from her hair and pressed it to her cheek, but as he moved in to kiss her, she gasped for air and jumped from his touch.

Holding his hands up in surrender, he watched as she gasped for air, much like she did the night she woke when Mrs. Winters' house was on fire.

"Abi. Honey, are you okay?"

She bent, placing her hands flat on the desk until she caught her breath. He moved to help her back up, but she shook her head. "Don't touch me."

"Okay," he agreed as he stepped back. "What did I do? What happened?"

Abigail turned her head. Her eyes were glossy from tears that had pooled. "I don't know. You touched me, and I saw something, but I don't know what it was. It got dark. There was dust everywhere, and I couldn't breathe."

"Is Mrs. Winters alright?" he asked, assuming she was still connected to her.

"I think so. I don't think that had anything to do with her."

"Maybe it has to do with my house. There's a lot of dust when I drywall or sand the floors."

She took in a few more breaths before nodding in agreement. "Maybe. Make sure all your windows are open."

"I will." He reached for her again, and she didn't react. "We're okay?"

"Carson, I didn't like that. My chest hurts."

"I'll take you to a hospital."

She shook her head. "No. I'm not sick. I'm not hurt. But I've never seen anything from your touch, except that one time when someone wanted to go after you and hurt you."

"You got me out of harm's way, remember?"

"I know," she said pressing her hand to her chest. "But this time I couldn't see where you were or what was happening."

"So you think that was me?"

He watched as she searched for an answer. "I don't know. Will you drive me home? I don't think I can drive now."

"Let me tell Emily and Mom that I'm leaving. There's nothing here that won't wait until Monday."

CARSON STOOD AT THE STOVE AND WAITED FOR THE WATER TO BOIL in the teapot. Abigail had opted for a few minutes alone to take a hot bath while he started a fire and brewed some tea.

He worried about what she'd seen when he touched her. No wonder she hated her sixth sense. Certainly, he didn't want anything to happen to him, but he didn't like what it did to her. That night when she woke up coughing as if she were in the fire with Mrs. Winters, that still played in his mind. How horrific. What did it do to her when she'd seen Katie Meadows dead in the river?

The teapot whistled, stirring him from his thoughts as Abigail walked out of the bedroom, her thick, white robe wrapped around her. She sat down on the couch and pulled a quilt up over her. Whatever she'd seen when he touched her had shaken her, he saw it on her face as she stared at the fire.

Carson poured each of them a cup of hot water and dropped in a tea bag. He wondered why she didn't have fancy tea at home, as she did at work. Perhaps the same reason he lived in a house that was in shambles. Work stayed at work for the most part.

She looked up at him as he set the cups on the coffee table and then sat down next to her. "Did the bath help?"

Abigail shrugged. "Did you call and check on Mrs. Winters? Nothing happened to her, right?"

"She's fine. Her family is fine. She's adjusting to her new place very well, Glenn said."

She nodded again. "I don't think we should see each other anymore," she said, and Carson had to take a moment to make sure he understood her correctly.

"You what?"

"It's too much. You're going to spend the rest of your life walking around on pins and needles with me. That's not fair to you. You deserve more than that. You need to go. You need to go now." Her voice rose as she spoke.

"Abigail, I don't want to go. I want to stay here with you. I love you, and in case you forgot, you love me too."

"It doesn't matter." She stood and moved away from him, wrapping her arms around herself. "You need to go on with your life. And I need to not be in it."

"And from what I've heard, that's not the case," he offered as he stood.

Abigail pushed her wet hair back from her face. "I'm making it how it is. If I can see the future, then I can change it. I got you out of the way once, and I can get you out again."

He took a step toward her, but when she stepped back, he stopped. "So breaking up with me is going to make it all better? I don't see how."

"It just is," she shouted as she turned her back to him. "Go. Go now."

What was he supposed to do with this? There was no way in hell he was going to leave her like this. And he sure as hell wasn't ready to give up on her altogether. He loved her, damnit, and it wasn't going to end like this.

"I'm going," he resigned. "I'm not giving up on us though. That's not going to happen. But when you're ready..."

"Go!" she shouted again.

Carson gathered his things and left her house again. He'd fix this. Somehow, he'd find a way.

CHAPTER 26

*A*bigail had told him to leave, and he had. But she didn't feel any better about the decision the next morning.

True to Colorado, the day before had been downright cold, and today was nearly seventy. Abigail decided she'd take that opportunity to clean up the garden in her backyard. Of course, snow was predicted for the next morning, and her birthday would be cold too.

Wasn't that the way of it? A day to celebrate, but it would be miserable. Surely Carson wouldn't think of bringing in Mrs. Winters to tea now, not after Abigail had been so horrible to him. But it was for his own good, or so she kept telling herself. In reality, it was probably best for her so she wouldn't have to see anything else when she touched him.

Abigail gathered tools from the shed. She would collect what was left of her garden, move a few pots into the covered patio, and it might give them a few weeks' worth of life. The leaves would be falling for weeks, but she would rake up the first set. Busy work was what she needed to calm her mind. So she got to it.

An hour into the yard work, she broke for a sandwich and

149

glass of water. Just as she was finishing her lunch, standing over the sink, she heard the knock on her front door. For a moment she stood there wondering if she could be quiet enough that whoever was would just go away. Her car was still parked at Carson's office, so they didn't have to know she was there. That was until she saw his mother's face peering around the corner of the front porch and catching her eye as Abigail stared out the window.

Patricia waved and held up a planter with orange and yellow mums.

Abigail tossed the remainder of her sandwich into the sink and headed toward the front door.

Patricia stood on Abigail's front porch, with a glorious smile on her face, holding the basket of mums. "I thought of you the moment I saw this and thought I would come over and bring them to you. Carson told me where you lived. I hope you don't mind."

There was no way Abigail could shoo the woman away. Her smile was infectious, and Abigail had a thing for fall flowers —damnit.

"Come on in," Abigail stood back from the door, and Patricia walked in.

Patricia looked around, as anyone would when they entered someone's home. "Your house is lovely. Carson's house is a mess, but you know that," she said, amusing herself with a laugh.

Abigail didn't take offense to the comment. She was sure it was small talk. "His house will be beautiful when he's done. I don't know where he'll find the time, but it will be beautiful."

"It would be better with a woman's touch," Patricia offered. She looked down at the basket in her hands. "I should hand these to you before I walk around the entire house with these in my hand, I hope you enjoy them."

Abigail took the flowers from Patricia. "They're lovely. I enjoy the fall color."

Patricia put her hand on her chest. "So do I. I have six of them on my porch. I had intended to put some of them on Mrs. Winters' porch, but the house is a mess. I have one more in my car, and I thought I would drop it off at her new place. I'm sure she would love some color."

"Can I offer you something to drink?" Abigail was sure the woman had come to stay longer than the time allotted to drop off the plant.

"I would love that."

"Come with me to the kitchen. We can sit out on the patio since it's nice out today."

Patricia nodded with a smile. "That sounds delightful. Carson told me all about your patio."

As they walked to the kitchen, Abigail wondered just what Carson had told his mother. Did she know that they had broken things off? If so, did she know why?

Abigail sat the flowers on the counter and pulled down two mugs. She turned to Patricia. "Would you like a cup of tea?"

"I love tea."

"It'll be just a few minutes. Feel free to have a seat at the table."

Patricia sat at the kitchen table and pulled off her jacket. She turned and hung it on the back of the chair, then crossed her legs and leaned forward as if to speak more intimately to Abigail.

"So your business is doing well?"

"Extremely well," she agreed as she filled the teapot with water, turned on the stove, and set the pot to boil. "Clare thinks it would be nice if we hired one more person. I'm not sure about that yet. I think perhaps we should wait. We do okay with just the two of us."

"Of course you do. But with the holidays coming, another hand might come in handy. I know Carson would be happy to help out on the weekends."

That statement said a lot. Maybe Carson hadn't told her anything.

"I suppose we'll have to see how busy we get." Abigail took her assorted basket of teas and set it on the table. "I don't keep the leaves here. Only bagged tea. I hope that's okay."

"Of course, sweetheart. I'm surprised you drink tea at home at all."

Abigail gave her a warm smile. "My obsession is real. Hence the shop. My grandmother loved tea. I suppose it's a tribute to her."

"And your grandmother has passed?"

Abigail nodded. "Yes. I miss her. I can only assume she sent me in the correct direction—career that is."

"I think your choice of careers is fabulous." Patricia looked through the teabags and pulled one out. "I always thought it would be fun to have a little shop downtown. I love the artisans and the unique gift shops. I think your tea shop is perfect there too."

It was interesting to Abigail, now, that she ever thought Carson was a tyrant. A tyrant wasn't raised by a woman like Patricia Stone. She was kind and thoughtful with her words. The gesture of showing up with flowers, that always meant a lot to Abigail. Carson simply was trying to make the place he lived in better. How come she didn't understand that before?

The teapot whistled on the stove, and Abigail turned to retrieve it. She carried it to the table and set it on the trivet which she kept there. As she did so, she caught Patricia's eye. There was something in the way that the woman looked at her. Was she scoping her out? Did she have more questions?

Abigail tended to always read too much into every situation. Who could blame her? She wanted to will her to go, but then again she enjoyed Patricia's company. It was like having her own mother sitting at her kitchen table, just for a visit.

"Which of these teas are your favorite?" Patricia asked.

"I'm very fond of the Egyptian licorice. It sounds a little funny, but it is my favorite."

Patricia looked at the bag that she had pulled from the basket, and she replaced it and pulled out an Egyptian licorice. "I think I'll try it. Shall we head to the patio?"

Abigail took a bag of tea from the basket and caught the enormous smile on Patricia's lips. Her heart ached for Carson now. Was that the reason behind this visit? She had to assume so, though she was thoroughly enjoying it.

CHAPTER 27

*A*bigail and Patricia had sat on the patio for nearly two hours. Abigail wondered how she could be comfortable with the woman. She assumed Carson had sent her, but by the time Patricia left, she had reconsidered.

Maybe Patricia just wanted to know about her. Was Carson that interested, she wondered as she washed the mugs they had drunk from. Of course, he was that interested, she justified. He had told her he loved her.

Patricia hadn't touched her or tried to hug her when she left. That made her consider that Carson had told her about that part of Abigail's life. Perhaps it was Abigail that had backed away if she thought there might be physical contact. After all, she was used to doing so, she hardly thought about it anymore.

She decided she should talk to Carson. If she went to his house, she would have that much time to decide whether to tell him to have his family leave her alone, or apologize for the way she acted. As she walked to her bedroom to change her clothes, she decided she wasn't going to apologize. There was nothing she was sorry for. Carson deserved better than what she could offer. However, perhaps they could be friends.

As she changed into a pair of jeans and slipped on a flowing cotton shirt, she considered the friends proposition. It sounded like every other breakup, but maybe this time he could be true. She didn't want him out of her life. But if she could change the course of history and not marry him, and not bring him any more drama, that would make her happy.

Abigail pulled her hair up into a ponytail and looked in the mirror. If she did this, she would be alone forever. If she turned away the man who loved her, and she needed to make a pact with herself to never fall in love again.

~

THE PHYSICAL LABOR OF BUILDING NEW SHELVES FOR THE LIVING room was exactly what Carson had needed today. He needed his thinking to be as clear as possible, and the grunt work made that happen.

As he stopped and took a sip of his water, his mind filled again with Abigail. He'd give her time. What else did he have but time? But he certainly wasn't giving up on her. Okay, so she had a crazy sixth sense, obviously so did other people. Who would've thought Mrs. Winters was one of them? Who else had this ability? Was he surrounded by people that could do this? And the nagging question in the back of his head, was what was going to happen to him? Why couldn't she see it?

He finished the bottle of water and threw the empty container in the trash. There were too many questions. The only answer to everything was to get back to work. He needed to keep progressing on the house and his projects.

He'd been in touch with the restaurateur who might be interested in the Ford Street church project if he could keep the church intact. Usually, that meant it was one of those people in the crowd, but Emily had done some digging. This guy was for real. And hadn't he already been thinking about keeping that building intact? Of course, he was going to do that for Abigail.

Carson let out a groan as he went back to what he was doing.

He lifted the brace for a shelf and leveled it in between the lines he had drawn. With one hand he managed nails from the pocket of his tool belt, resting them between his teeth, and then retrieved his hammer. Once the brace looked even, he skillfully managed the nail into place, but as he swung the hammer, he hit his hand instead.

The shock of it had him dropping the brace and hammer, and falling off the step-ladder to the floor. The impact jarred him as he hit his head on the floor.

"Mother...." He screamed as he heard another scream from the door.

"Carson!" Abigail dropped the bags in her hand and ran to him. "Oh, God! Are you okay? Don't move. Let me look at you. Let me..."

Perhaps he was dazed and confused, but looking up into her eyes made all the pain go away. "I'm fine," he interrupted her. "God, you're beautiful."

"Carson, this isn't the time for..."

He cut her off again by reaching for her and pulling her atop of him. Covering her mouth with his took the pain from his fall, and the disaster of a day, and lightened it. She'd come to him. She was here.

A moment later, she pulled back from him and stood. The glazed-over caring look was gone and had been replaced with anger.

"Stop it!" she demanded. "Just stop."

Carson sat up and quickly placed his hand on the back of his head to ease the throbbing. "Shit!"

"Are you hurt?"

"Yes."

"Good," she said through gritted teeth as she crossed her arms in front of her. "You should be more careful."

"Got it."

"You should watch what you're doing."

"Thought I was."

"You're an idiot."

And that one didn't need a response, he thought.

Carson eased himself to his knees, then took a breath to steady himself before he stood. Replacing his hand to the back of his head he looked at her standing before him, her cheeks red with anger. "What are you doing here?"

"I brought you groceries," she said as she looked toward the door at the mess of milk and eggs oozing from the bags. "What a mess." She hurried toward the mess, and he followed. "Well, get a trash can. All you have left is squished bread for sandwiches."

He didn't move right away. Instead, he opted to watch her fuss over groceries she'd brought for an idiot. What kind of woman did that?

Carson went to the kitchen and brought back the trash can and a roll of paper towel. With his head pounding, and his hand bruising, he knelt down next to her and helped clean up the mess.

"Why did you bring me groceries?"

"Because I'm nervous."

Carson sat back on his heels and watched her. "You're nervous?"

Abigail stopped mopping up crushed eggs to study him. "Yes. Is that such a surprise?"

"Yes," he answered honestly. "Why would you be nervous around me?"

"Because I broke things off with you."

"Right, so why the groceries?"

Now she sat back on her heels, her knees wet from spilled milk. "Why did you send your mother over to my house?"

"Why did I..." Carson stopped and let out a long breath. "I

didn't send her over. Damnit. I told her I was home because we, well, because things were strained between us, is what I told her. I'm sorry I didn't know she'd go to your house. That had to be uncomfortable."

Abigail remained silent for a moment. "It was very nice actually." She tossed the soiled paper towel into the trash can and pulled more off the roll. "She didn't let on that she knew we'd," she paused, "broken things off."

"You broke them off."

"It's best."

"For you," he argued. "I don't like it."

"Well…"

Again, she was speechless.

Carson reached for her hand and pulled her up with him, and away from the mess. He led her to the bedroom, which was the only place to sit.

Abigail took a seat on the bed, and Carson remained standing watching her as if she were processing something deep inside of her.

"Abi, if we're done, why are you here?"

"I told you. I wanted to know why your mother came by."

"And that included groceries?"

Her lips pursed. "I told you. I was nervous."

Carson raked his fingers through his hair. "I didn't send my mother. She likes you. She probably wanted to make sure you were alright if things between us were stressed. I'll let her know to leave you alone."

Abigail looked down at her clenched hands in her lap. "I don't want that at all, Carson. In fact, I came here to make sure we can be friends."

"Friends? You want to be friends?" He shrugged his hands in the air. "If that's all I get, then I guess I can settle. But that's not what I want, Abigail. It's not what I want at all."

"I can't give you the prediction. I can't go on thinking that you love me, or will marry me because I said I saw it. And I can't go on worried every single day that what I see, or don't see, could hurt you."

Carson moved to the bed and sat down next to her. He took her hand and linked their fingers together. When she tried to tug away, he held on tighter.

"All of this hurts, Abigail. I don't know what deep dark hole you saw me in, but I feel like I'm in it. It's premature, and I think I want to marry you. And I've never felt like that before with anyone." When she took a breath to say something, he lifted a finger to her lips to silence her. "That's not a proposal. You don't deserve some mid-fight proposal. You deserve better. But I can't keep you if you don't want to be kept. It's obvious my family loves you, and you know that I love you. All that's left is for you to decide that I'm worthy of your trust and that I can deal with your gift."

ABIGAIL LOOKED AT THEIR HANDS LOCKED TOGETHER. SHE SAW nothing. But she felt everything.

"I do trust you," she admitted as her voice shook. "I just don't want you to have to deal with it."

"It's no different than you going to a community meeting and everyone turning against me. I don't want you to deal with that."

Abigail chuckled. "It gets pretty ugly."

"It always does."

"And how do you deal with that? Personally, I mean."

"I believe in what I do. Real estate development is an opportunity. Sometimes that opportunity comes at a price to the area. I get it. No matter what I choose to build in my life, there's going to be somebody who's against it. Just like your gift," he said as he lifted his other hand to her cheek. "I get that the town you lived in turned against you. I understand it. I thought you were crazy that night telling me to leave and go to Mrs. Winters' house. But what would have happened if I hadn't gone with you? I don't even want to think about it."

Abigail touched the hand that lingered on her face. "I don't want to see you hurt. Something inside me still tells me you're going to get hurt."

Carson laughed. "I did get hurt, damnit. You hurt my heart. Then I bruised my hand and fell on my head."

Abigail snickered and covered her lips with her fingers. "Do you think that was all it was?"

"I have no idea, and I don't know. Each day is a gift, and I want to experience it just like that. I want to unwrap it and see what's inside. All your gift did was shake the present. We found each other. And if you'll have me, I'll watch my step every day. I don't want to lose you, Abi. If fate says you are my soulmate, then I've got to believe it."

"That fate shows me four kids." She let out an unsteady breath. "How do we deal with that?"

"All I heard you say was that we need to practice," he said as he lowered her back on the bed and took her mouth passionately with his.

CHAPTER 28

The nicest table in the tea shop was near the window on the west side of the store. It opened up to Lookout Mountain.

Abigail had set it special for Mrs. Winters' birthday celebration, with three chairs. She'd found the Prussian china sets, which she loved the most, and used them for presentation. Clare had arranged an elegant tea, and Abigail had ordered an ornate flower arrangement with roses, which had been delivered that morning.

The antique store down the street had had a crystal tiara in the window, and Abigail couldn't help herself. She bought it for Mrs. Winters and had it on the table waiting with the arrangement.

She hadn't seen Mrs. Winters since they had visited in the hospital, though Carson assured her she was doing fantastic in her new place. As she primped in the small office space, in the back of the store, Clare leaned against the doorjamb and watched her.

"You look happy, Abi. Really happy," she said as Abigail fussed with her curls, and then touched up her lipstick.

"I want to be happy," Abigail said. "I guess I'm glad he's so stubborn."

That caused Clare to laugh. "You're a good team that way."

Abigail chose not to take the stab at her personality seriously. Of course she was stubborn. She had to be. However, had he not been so stubborn, then they would have missed this opportunity.

The chimes above the door rang and Clare looked behind them through the kitchen. "Your party is here," she told Abigail as she went back to work on pastries.

Abigail took one more look at herself in the mirror. Maybe she did look happy. Had she seriously forgotten what it looked like?

She looked down at her dress and realized she still had on her apron. Taking it off, she hung it on the hook as she was going to sit down and enjoy this tea even if she was the host.

The moment she turned the corner from the kitchen, she caught Carson's eye. The smile that developed on his face told her that he loved her as much as he said he did. It gave her heart a little kick each time.

Mrs. Winters was removing her jacket, with Carson's help. As soon as she was free from it, she turned to see Abigail standing there.

"Abigail, happy birthday." She held open her arms and waited for Abigail to move to her.

Though Abigail wouldn't even think of not hugging the woman, fear bubbled in her throat as she wondered what she would see.

Abigail moved to Mrs. Winters and let her hug her. Squeezing her eyes shut, Abigail forced any foreign thoughts from her mind.

Mrs. Winters stepped back and examined her. "You look lovely."

"As do you," Abigail complimented. "I do believe you're glowing."

Mrs. Winters leaned in toward Abigail's ear. "I'll tell you a secret. I was wrong to live alone in the house for so many years. It's fantastic to live among others." She stepped back and smiled.

Carson pulled out a chair. "Mrs. Winters, why don't you sit here," he offered.

Mrs. Winters took the seat, and Carson turned toward Abigail.

He took her hands in his and kissed her on the cheek. "Happy birthday, beautiful."

Mrs. Winters let out a grumble. "Dear Lord, boy. Kiss her correctly. You can't love a woman and not kiss her correctly on her birthday," she scolded.

Abigail felt the heat rise in her cheeks as Carson tipped his head and placed a kiss on her lips which lingered until every cell in her body buzzed with the delight that his kisses brought to her.

"There are three chairs. I assume you're joining us?"

Abigail nodded. "Yes. Clare has taken care of everything."

Carson pulled out the chair next to Mrs. Winters, and Abigail sat down. Carson then took the remaining seat.

Mrs. Winters admired the floral arrangement. "These are lovely, my dear."

"They're for you," Abigail acknowledged. "I know you love roses."

"I most certainly do."

"And the box there is for you as well," she offered as Mrs. Winters reached for the wrapped box.

"You got me a present?" she asked, and Abigail noticed Carson's glance toward her.

"I did. I saw it on my way to work this morning, and you had to have it."

Mrs. Winters reached for her and patted her hand, which to Abigail's delight, did not share any visions with her.

Mrs. Winters went on to rip open the wrapping like a child at Christmas, which delighted Abigail. When she pulled the crystal tiara from the box, she laughed the most joyous laugh Abigail had ever heard from an adult.

"Oh, my! This is the most delightful thing I've ever seen. Thank you."

Carson sat back in his chair and crossed his legs, as he did when he observed. "That's a fantastic present, Abigail. Mrs. Winters certainly is our queen."

"Maybe she's a princess," Abigail countered.

Mrs. Winters laughed. "Oh, I'm a queen. Most definitely a queen. And dear, Abigail, you can be my princess."

Abigail smiled. "I'd like that."

"Carson, come put this on me. I want to wear it every day."

Carson stood and walked to Mrs. Winters. He took the tiara from her and placed it on her head. "Does that feel right?"

"It feels perfect. I feel like royalty. Thank you, Abigail. This was a fantastic surprise."

As Carson rounded Abigail's chair, he ran his fingers across her shoulders, and she stiffened. Again, her head filled with a dark cloud, but she couldn't see anything inside of it. She tried to keep her reaction neutral, though she was sure that Mrs. Winters already knew she'd seen something.

Clare bounded from the kitchen with a tray of tea pots for each of them.

Abigail looked at Mrs. Winters. "I don't think you've met my cousin Clare yet. Clare, this is Mrs. Winters."

Clare set the tray on the table next to them and shook Mrs. Winters' hand. "It's a pleasure to meet you. These two talk about you often."

"They should," she said. "I'm the one who brought them together." She looked at Abigail and then to Carson. "I think they'll live happily ever after." She assured them with her eyes.

Carson's hand slipped under the table and to Abigail's knee. She turned to look at him smiling at her. She certainly did love him, even if this budding romance was new. Thank goodness they'd worked through her insecurities, she thought as Clare began to explain their tea for the afternoon.

Of course, Abigail didn't hear Clare's description of anything as she was busy thinking about the man, whose hand caressed her thigh. Perhaps Mrs. Winters was right to marry her love when she knew he was right. They'd have arguments and disagreements again, but he'd stood by her side every time she tried to push him away.

"Abi."

She looked up at Carson to see that he was talking to her. "Sorry, what did you say?"

"I asked you to hand me the cream."

"Oh," she said as she nodded and handed it to him.

"Are you okay? You looked a bit lost for a moment."

Abigail looked at Mrs. Winters, and then back at Carson. "I was just thinking about what Mrs. Winters said about us and happily ever after."

Carson poured the cream into his tea, then set it on the table. "And what were you thinking about it?"

Abigail let out a breath as she took Carson's hand. "I was thinking that I was glad we worked things out, and I'm thankful that you're not foolish enough to always listen to me. Not everyone is going to cower from me and what I can see. You're both proof of that," she said as she sent a smile toward Mrs. Winters. "I love you. And I'm glad that she saw that too."

Carson leaned in and pressed a kiss to her lips. "I'm glad she did too. Now, Clare said she made a cake for you ladies. I can't wait to try it."

As Abigail watched Clare bring out the cake she'd been fussing over, and Mrs. Winters' eyes went wide with a child-like wonder, Abigail realized that everything was going to be perfect for them. It truly was a spectacular birthday so far, and she was glad to be sharing it with Mrs. Winters and the man she loved.

CHAPTER 29

*C*arson lay awake as Abigail slept in his arms. Her naked body conformed to his, and her breath was light on his skin. She smelled sweet, he thought, as he ran his hand over her hair. The dainty diamond earrings he'd given her for her birthday sparkled in the moonlight. She'd cried when she opened them, but quickly put them on. No one had ever given her jewelry before, and that surprised him. She deserved pretty things, and he very much wanted to be the man to give them to her.

His mind wandered to the last lunch he had with Mrs. Winters. He'd had reservations at the Golden Hotel, and she'd been adamant he change them so they could go to the tea shop. Thank God she had been.

This woman, whom he was afraid to let go of, had been waiting for him in that little shop. He could never have imagined that his life would change that day.

He thought about what he'd been told of visions she and Mrs. Winters had about them. The smile that tugged at his lips was directly related to him thinking about them having four children. It was a bit overwhelming, but at the same time exhilarating.

Would they have sons or daughters? With four, they probably

had a few of each. Abigail would be a wonderful mother. Would he be a good father?

He'd had an attentive father—yeah, he'd make sure he was the perfect father.

What would his children think of his career? Would they assume he only tore down beautiful things, or would they understand the necessity of it? He couldn't help but wonder if Abigail had come to understand it. She hadn't mentioned the church project for a while, and he hadn't told her about the changes he'd been considering.

The community meeting had been postponed due to the newest developments. Everything still hinged on whether or not the building could be physically secured before they began. Either way, things needed to start moving. The building needed to come down, or it needed to be started before someone, usually transients or kids, got inside and got hurt.

Abigail stirred in his arms, and Carson pressed a kiss to her forehead.

He thought about how new their relationship was. They'd only been together for a month, and here they'd been living with each other, for the most part. They already knew their fate was sealed, and they'd be married. Was there an actual time for that? Was he supposed to wait to ask her to marry him and how was he to know when?

Pressing another kiss to her head, he realized that Mrs. Winters would have all of those answers. He'd decided it was time to ask them. He was absolutely sure that Abi was the one woman he wanted to spend his whole life with.

THE OFFICE BUZZED WITH A NEW PROJECT, AND THAT WAS WHAT Carson enjoyed about his work. A developer had just purchased an old office building, and he wanted to convert it into offices, condos, and shopping.

Carson and Doug had toured the building that morning and had just finished meeting with the developer. Doug had gone straight to work on getting drawings started, and Carson followed up on emails about the Ford Street church.

The restaurateur had contacted him with a list of questions and design thoughts, which Carson was running by the engineers on the project.

As his day had crept into afternoon, and he felt the fatigue of his job settle into him, he opened a Coke from the mini-fridge in his office and took a long, satisfying swig.

He could certainly use the caffeine jolt today. The night had been short, though some of that was because he'd made love to the woman he loved all night. The rest of it was the thoughts that had kept him awake racing through his mind.

Carson looked at the clock again. It was almost three-thirty. He wouldn't hear from the engineers until tomorrow, and Doug would be in his office working solidly on the new project. This was the perfect time to visit Mrs. Winters, he decided.

AFTER TELLING EMILY AND HIS MOTHER THAT HE WAS LEAVING early, he headed to the facility where Mrs. Winters now lived. He was happy Glenn had chosen that specific assisted living facility, as it had been one that Carson had helped design.

He wasn't surprised to find Mrs. Winters in the commons area, surrounded by other women, laughing and sharing stories. He couldn't help but wonder if she shared her gift with them by telling them things as if she were fortune telling.

Lingering in the doorway, he watched as she held the hand of a woman in a wheelchair. He couldn't hear what she told her, but the woman nodded as Mrs. Winters spoke and then hugged her.

"Is that your mother?" A male nurse moved to stand next to Carson.

"No, just a dear friend," he said as he watched her laugh with another woman.

"She's very popular. Seems to have a sixth sense or something. Lots of the people here do. I think it comes to them when they get older."

Carson turned to the man. "Do you mean they have it or they think they have it."

The nurse laughed. "When I first started in elder care, I would have said they made crap up. You know, just to humor themselves. But I've seen stuff around here that makes the hair on the back of your neck stand up. They know what they're talking about."

Carson knew that was true—especially where Mrs. Winters was concerned. And as if that sixth sense kicked in, Mrs. Winters looked toward the door and saw him standing there with the nurse. She waved him in.

He walked to her, taking her outstretched hands, and then kissing her cheek.

"This is the man I told you all about. The best friend of my late Jeffery. He's a wonderful addition to our family," she shared as she patted his cheek. "Carson, why don't you escort me back to my room."

She stood and took his arm.

"You're looking fantastic," he said as they walked slowly down the hall toward her room.

"Days are numbered."

When she spoke like that his heart ached. "Well, you wouldn't know it to look at you."

He couldn't argue with her. After all, she could see the future. He couldn't.

Mrs. Winters went right to her chair and eased back. "Ah, I'm glad they salvaged this from my house. It's like home."

Carson wasn't sure what to say to that. He pulled up a chair from the small table by the window and sat down. "It looks like you're making friends here."

She shrugged at that. "Carson, they are so lonely. People put their loved ones in places like this and forget about them. My family comes every day. You visit. Abigail visits. You know..."

He held up a hand. "Abi has been here?"

His question seemed to stump her. "Well, wait." She thought for a moment. "No, I guess she hasn't. But I talk to her every day. She might not know that."

And for the first time, he thought Mrs. Winters had lost her mind.

"What do you mean you talk to her, but she doesn't know?"

Mrs. Winters brushed away his comment with her hand. "You're looking at me like I'm a crazy old woman."

"I'm sorry."

"No, you're not, but you're beginning to understand it. She's scared, Carson. I've lived a long time to know that people begin to ignore warnings and assume you're a nut job. She's just learning it. She doesn't want to mess up her business or her relationship. And she's very against you tearing down that church," she added.

He smiled. "I'm trying to keep it intact," he said, letting her in on his secret. "I want her to know that it means that much to me."

Mrs. Winters reached for his hand but pulled back with the same look Abigail had when they were at the tea shop. She studied him for a long moment, and the joy which had filled her eyes when she'd seen him had clouded over.

"Be careful, Carson. Remember there was a reason you wanted that building to be redone in the first place."

"It's unstable. I have engineers working on it."

That seemed to ease her as she sat back in her chair. "So, why are you here in the middle of your day? You're a busy man."

"Never too busy for my best girl."

She smiled. "I'm second best now."

"Never." Carson leaned forward with his arms on his thighs. "I did want to ask you something. Abi and I haven't been together very long. A month. But we've exchanged words. We've slept in each other's beds. I know how she likes her tea, her toast, and what she puts on pizza. I've decided I want to marry her."

The smile on Mrs. Winters' lips grew wider. "That's always been in the plan."

"Right. But when? I can't believe I'm saying this, but I'm ready now. However, I don't think she is, even though she knows it's in the plan. When should I ask her? What do I do?"

Mrs. Winters closed her eyes. "You'll know, darling. There will be a moment, and it will be the right moment."

He'd certainly been hoping for more than that.

When Mrs. Winters didn't open her eyes, he leaned in closer. She had fallen asleep. She'd always been able to run the conversation in her favor, he thought as he kissed his fingertips and pressed them to her cheek. He was a lucky man to have such a woman in his life.

CHAPTER 30

The adjustments Carson had requested for the Ford Street church had come back, and it wasn't what he'd wanted to hear at all. Though the exterior could be saved, the building itself was unsafe. In order to keep it intact, the price just doubled, and the time frame in which he'd promised the city he'd have it done had extended too.

Carson leaned back in his office chair, folding his hands behind his head. He'd spent all night thinking about how he wanted to propose to Abigail, and when. His focus had been to do it when the church was safe enough to go into. Now it looked like that would be many months away, and he wasn't sure he wanted to wait that long.

He chuckled to himself, as he lowered his arms and moved back to his desk. The church project had been so important to him, and now it completely revolved around what Abigail thought about it. That was true love, right? When a man lost his ever loving mind and compromised his business to see the woman he loved smile?

With a grin still on his face, he went back to work on the plans as his mother strolled through the door.

"Have you seen what Abigail has done with her shop?" His mother set a large gift bag in the chair on the other side of his desk.

"Good or bad?"

"Oh, my goodness! Good. I didn't know Halloween decor could be classy. She's genius. And the pastries her cousin has come up for the season; genius too."

Pride swelled inside of him as if he'd been the one to create his mother's mood over the cute things Abigail did to her store. "What do you have?"

"Gifts. I bought assorted teas, mugs, tea sets, and some linens she just got in. The ladies in my book club want to start meeting there each month, so I went in to set that up. Carson, she's so fantastic."

Did his mother even realize how she sounded gushing over his girlfriend? That was a good sign, he decided.

"Mom, sit down," he said as he stood and moved to the door. "I want to talk to you about something."

His mother watched him carefully as he closed the door. "Oh, you didn't have another argument did you? Carson, what's wrong with…"

"No argument, Mom. Sit down. I want to show you something."

Hesitantly, his mother moved the bag from the chair and sat down. Carson moved to his desk and opened his center drawer. He pulled out a ring box and slid it across the top of the desk.

His mother's eyes went wide. "What is that?"

"Open it. I want to know what you think."

He saw his mother's hand shake as she picked it up and opened it.

A moment later he saw the tears pool in her eyes and begin to leave trails down her cheek.

"Now, why are you crying?" he asked as he pulled a tissue from the box on his desk and handed it to her.

"This is for Abigail? You're going to give it to her?"

Carson walked around his desk and stood in front of his mother before he sat on his desk. "I was thinking about it."

"Oh, Carson. This is... I mean..." She pressed the tissue to her nose as she looked at the diamond set in rose gold. "It's lovely. She's going to adore it."

He took the box back from his mother and looked at it. "I hope she does."

"You're going to ask her to marry you?"

With a nod and a smile, he looked at his mother. "Yes. I love her. I know it's quick, but I..."

"You know it's right. Oh, Carson," she said as she stood and wrapped her arms around him. "I'm so happy for you."

As his mother stepped back, he closed the box. "Now, don't go telling anyone."

"Lips are sealed," she said as she mimicked zippering them.

"I called her mother this morning and arranged a time to talk to her father on Skype. I won't do anything until I have their blessing."

"Don't you think you should go out there and meet them."

Carson pursed his lips. "I thought about that. I'm sure she would want me to do that too. But I don't want to wait to ask her."

His mother rested her hand on his cheek. "You always were a go-getter. I'm very happy for you. I love her, and you know I love you."

"Thanks, Mom. That means a lot."

Picking up her gift bag, she turned and let out a sigh. "I can't tell your father?"

Carson narrowed his gaze at her, and she laughed.

"I won't tell him. You're right. He can't keep a secret."

She blew him a kiss as she let herself out of the office. Carson put the ring back into his drawer.

With a smile on his face, he got back to work. He was very

grateful for his mother's reaction. Everyone loved Abigail. He was one lucky man.

~

THE PUMPKIN AND WITCH-SHAPED COOKIES, WHICH CLARE HAD made that morning, had sold out by noon. She'd already started her next batch as Abigail cleared a table for a walk-in tea.

In the past two weeks, Abigail noted, business had picked up significantly. Perhaps she'd been wrong when she told Patricia Stone that she and Clare could handle everything. They just might have to hire someone after all.

"I can clear tables in ten minutes," Clare said as Abigail set up a tray for the walk-in.

"Thanks. I don't know if we got onto some website, or if people are just getting out and about lately. I don't think we've ever been this busy."

Clare laughed. "Maybe it's your future mother-in-law. She's got her book club here. How much did she spend here this morning?"

"I'm not going to brag about that," Abigail said as she lifted the tray and dropped it back to the counter as she pressed her hand to her chest and fought for breath.

"Abi!" Clare moved to her. "Oh, God! Are you having a heart attack? What's wrong?"

"I'm fine. I'm fine!" Abigail scolded as she caught her breath. "I just couldn't breathe. My head is a little fuzzy, and I can't catch my breath."

"You need help," Clare said as she moved to the phone.

"Don't you call anyone. I'm fine," Abigail argued as she gained control.

Clare studied her for a moment. "You're color is coming back. Did you eat breakfast or lunch?"

"Yes."

"Do you have a cold?"

"No."

Clare's eyes grew wide as she moved to Abigail and took her hands. "Are you pregnant?" she whispered.

Abigail pulled her hands back and brushed them off on the front of her apron. "I got my period two days ago. No. I'm not pregnant."

She went back to fixing the tray under Clare's watchful eye. She was steady as she picked up the tray again and carried it out to the table. No one beyond the kitchen was any the wiser, and Abigail served tea and scones with a smile. But even she had to wonder what that was all about.

CHAPTER 31

*B*ecause Carson's house was still not fully finished, though the kitchen was coming along, they'd agreed to stay at Abigail's.

She'd stopped and bought groceries and had planned a nice meal. Though not much of a cook, she could roast a chicken just fine with potatoes and vegetables.

The audible appreciation was heard from Carson the moment he walked through the door. "God, that smells good," he said as he closed the front door and walked into the kitchen.

Abigail opened a bottle of wine and poured two glasses, as he came up behind her and wrapped his arms around her waist. His lips went straight to her neck, and she relaxed against him. "I'm glad you're home."

"Me too. It was a long day," he said as she handed him one of the glasses and took the other for herself. "You're doing okay though?"

Abigail set her glass on the counter and turned to him. "What is that supposed to mean?"

"Only asking."

"Who told you what?"

He sipped his wine before setting his glass next to hers and taking her hands. "Clare called me, and before you get mad," he held waited for her to relax and not speak. "I'm glad she did. I think you're stressing a lot at work and about us. I thought maybe we could take a long weekend and you could take me home with you and show me around."

"No," she said quickly and hoped that it carried the right tone to make her point.

Carson continued to hold her hands as he processed her answer. "Don't you think your family would like to see you?"

"They will at Thanksgiving when they come out here. I'm not going back, Carson. Not now. Not ever."

She turned from him hoping he'd leave it at that, but when he turned her back to him, she knew that wasn't going to hold him.

"I know that the people there treated you poorly. I get that. But, seriously, enough that you won't ever go back?"

Abigail felt the tears burning in her throat, and she fought them back. "No. Not ever. Now, I've made us a delightful dinner. Can we enjoy our wine and our dinner?"

Carson pulled her to him and kissed the top of her head. "I love you."

"I love you, too, and I need you to understand."

"I'm trying." He stepped back but kept his hands on her arms. "Tell me you're not sick. Tell me you're not stressed. And tell me you're okay, and I'll believe you."

"I'm fine. Nothing is wrong with me. I just got dizzy at the store. We are super busy, but I'm not stressed. Is that good enough?"

"I guess it will have to be. I'd still like to take a weekend, just you and me."

Abigail rested her hand on his chest. "It'll have to wait until the beginning of the new year. The holidays will be very busy for us."

"Okay. I'll make some plans for the new year."

She pressed her hand to his cheek and felt as though she had his word. He would let her be until then.

CARSON DECIDED NOT TO PUSH THE ISSUE OF WHAT CLARE HAD told him for the rest of the night. Abigail seemed content to serve dinner, take the offered help to clean up after, and then to sit and watch When Harry Met Sally on TV. As he listened to Harry and Sally reminisce about how they met, Carson thought about his house and her house. Neither was big enough for four kids, but just because he was told they'd have four kids, no one said they'd all come at the same time. If she did accept his proposal, he had to assume they'd move into her house, and eventually, he'd contract to have his finished. The thought humored him. Maybe when they were ready for a bigger house, he could have a hand in building it.

There was no denying that he was a bit disappointed when Clare confirmed that Abigail wasn't pregnant. He never thought that a slip up like that would be welcomed, but it most certainly would be.

She looked up at him when he realized he'd given her a squeeze with his arm as she cuddled up to him.

"What are you thinking about?" she asked. Her voice soft.

"Our future. I think about it a lot."

"Me too. And I think Mrs. Winters is right. Ellie is a nice name for a girl."

He pressed another kiss to the top of her head. "You'd do that? Name a daughter Ellie?"

"Of course. What better story to have than to tell people you're named after the woman to brought your parents together."

Carson pulled her to him even tighter now. "I think we should tell her our plans. I think it'll lift her spirits."

∼

THEY PLANNED THEIR SPECIAL VISIT TO MRS. WINTERS FOR EARLY the next morning, before work. When they arrived, they found her, again, surrounded by people in the dining hall having her breakfast.

She rose, and walked to them, enveloping them both in a hug, which Abigail felt surge through her.

"What a wonderful sight. I'm done with my breakfast. Let's take a walk to the game room. It has a nice view." Mrs. Winters hooked her arm through one from each of them and started toward the game room. "I had a feeling you two would come today, and I'm so glad you did."

"So not a huge surprise, huh?" Carson patted her hand which was hooked on his arm. "You're no fun at Christmas are you?"

Mrs. Winters laughed. "Oh, it's fun for me. You've never bought me something I didn't love. How do you suppose that happened?"

"Until this moment, I assumed I was a good gift giver."

Abigail laughed at his expense, and he shifted a glance her way.

Mrs. Winters rested her head against his shoulder as they walked down the hallway. "I talk to you, too, when you sleep. You just don't know it either," she said, and Abigail wondered if she talked to her, too. Lately, Mrs. Winters had been on her mind a lot. She wanted to ask her about the dizzy spells and the black cloud vision, but not in front of Carson. With it being the only vision she had with Carson, she was sure it was bad.

They walked into the room, with the western view of the mountains, and sat down at one of the card tables. The room was empty since it was still breakfast.

"I designed this part of the facility myself," Carson said as he looked around. "Donated most of the games, too."

Mrs. Winters patted his hand. "I'm sure that's why they chose this facility to put me in. I miss my house though." She pulled back her hand and adjusted the bracelets on her wrist.

"Glenn says it's going to be a great while before it's livable. I think he's full of horse crap," she offered, and Abigail stifled a laugh.

Carson leaned back in his chair and crossed a leg over the other. "Why do you say that?"

"Because I'm old. I'm losing my mind. And I'm going to die. He doesn't want me to do that in my house."

The laugh that had been present shifted and nearly choked Abigail when she heard that. "This is a wonderful facility," she added hoping that her voice hadn't shaken as she felt it had.

"It's nice. I'll die here," Mrs. Winters said as she looked around the room. "I've seen it." The words were so nonchalant Abigail wondered if she were already ready to pass on. She didn't look it or sound it. Would she too get to that point sometime in her life?

Carson shook his head. "I hope for the first time, you're wrong."

Mrs. Winters simply gave him a grunt. "Why did you come this morning?"

Carson reached across the table for Abigail's hand. "We've been talking."

"You didn't propose. I can tell."

He smiled. "No. But we've been talking about the future. I know she's in it," he said with a wink in Abigail's direction that had her heart flutter. "I've been told we will have four children too."

Mrs. Winters again gave him a grunt which worried Abigail. Was that a wrong premonition? Or was four not enough? That was one thing she didn't even want to know about.

The smile on Carson's mouth widened. "Anyway, we both agreed that when we have a daughter, we will name her Ellie, after you."

Mrs. Winters clapped her hands together, causing her bracelets to chime on her wrists. "Oh, that makes me so happy. She'll be spirited. I promise you that."

Carson gave Abigail's hand a squeeze. "I have no doubt," he said.

Mrs. Winters reached for Abigail's free hand, and Abigail saw a flash in her eyes. The worry that clouded them was quickly covered by a smile. "Your grandmother would like one named after her too. Gwendolyn is a beautiful name."

The tears that had threatened earlier burst through and Abigail pulled back both of her hands to quickly wipe them away.

"I never told you my grandmother's name," she said to Mrs. Winters.

"You didn't have to, honey. She told me."

Abigail's heart raced as tears continued to stream down her cheeks.

"Carson, go to my room. In the top drawer of my dresser, there is an embroidered handkerchief. Bring it to Abigail. I want her to have it. My mother made it," she said, instructing him.

"I'll be right back," he said as he stood and left the room.

Abigail brushed away the tears and willed them to dry as Mrs. Winters turned to her. The humor and grace had left her face, which now grew pale.

"The church. Stop him."

Abigail swallowed hard trying grasp what she was saying. "I've been trying to stop him from…"

"All of it." Mrs. Winters voice shook. "He can't be part of it. Make him sell it. Make him—he has to stop." The words were stern and defined.

A nurse came to the door. "Ellie, I've been sent for you. You have a hair appointment."

The color returned to Mrs. Winter's cheeks, as did the smile as she turned to Abigail. "My son spoils me by paying for hair appointments." She looked back at the nurse. "Okay. I'm ready."

She stood, and the nurse hurried to her side.

"Goodbye, Abigail. Take care of my boy. I love you," she said as they walked out of the room.

Abigail sat there alone, her heart pounding in her chest and tears choking her. The desperation that had taken over Mrs. Winters' face still sat with her. What more was there to that church that could hurt Carson? Why was she warning her?

A moment later Carson walked back in with the handkerchief.

"It looks like you could still use this."

He handed it to her, and she looked at it. White linen with lace trim and a butterfly embroidered on the corner. "This is lovely."

Carson nodded and knelt down next to her chair. He ran his hand up her arm as if to soothe her. "I passed Mrs. Winters in the hallway. She told me to take care of you."

As Abigail dabbed her eyes with the handkerchief, she smiled up at him. "She told me to do the same for you."

CHAPTER 32

*T*he wind picked up as the sun tucked itself away behind the mountains. Forecasters were calling for an October snow.

Carson built a fire as Abigail filled bowls of chili from the slow cooker. He thought about how cozy her home was, and how welcome he felt there. Would tonight be a good time to give her the ring?

No, he decided. Her mind had been elsewhere since their visit with Mrs. Winters. He'd wait. They'd have many romantic nights together for him to choose from.

Another thought crossed his mind. Perhaps it would raise her spirits if he told her about his plans for the church project. Wouldn't she love to know that they were working on saving it? Yes, that would ease whatever was on her mind. He was sure of it.

Carson picked up the bottle of wine he had set on the coffee table and opened it. He poured them each a glass. As he corked the bottle, he watched Abigail move about the kitchen.

She was an angel that had happened into his life—thanks to Mrs. Winters, of course. But after a month, he couldn't imagine another day going by where she wasn't part of it. He wasn't sure how much longer he could hold off on his proposal. The thought that she might shoot him down petrified him. It was safer to wait until he was sure she'd say yes.

Abigail walked into the living room with a tray he recognized to be one like the ones she had at the tea shop. On it, she had two bowls, spoons, crackers, cheese, and sour cream. She certainly had thought of everything.

"I'm out of butter," she said as she set the tray down.

"Butter? We're having chili."

She lifted her eyes to him and a crease formed between her brows. "You don't put butter on your crackers?"

"I crumble crackers."

"Yes, with butter on them?"

Carson laughed. "No. I've never heard of such a thing. I guess that's unique to you."

A smile slipped across her pink lips. "No. It's a thing." Abigail set the tray on the table, and he quickly caught her hand and pulled her down onto the couch, trapping her under him.

She giggled at him, which set his heart rate higher. "What are you doing?"

"I just needed to kiss you," he said lowering his mouth to hers and tasting the sweetness of her.

"Our dinner will get cold," she protested as he moved his lips to her throat.

Carson let out a groan as he propped himself up, hovering over her. "Later then. But I wanted to tell you how much I love you."

Her eyes softened with his words. "I love you too."

"It makes me very happy to hear you say that." He sat back and helped her up. "Thanks for making dinner."

"Just remember, if you're planning a life with me, you won't eat like a king."

"Oh, I don't know about that. Food isn't the focus. Having you by my side forever is the focus."

The smile remained on her lips as she set a bowl in front of each of them. She handed him a linen napkin and draped one over her own lap before she began doctoring her chili—sans butter, which he figured he'd never understand.

Carson picked up his bowl after adding an ample amount of cheese and crushing crackers into it. "So, I wanted to tell you about a project I'm working on."

Abigail was dainty with her addition of cheese and a few crackers, which she crushed with her spoon, and not her hand. "Oh, yeah? A new one?"

"No, not exactly. The Ford Street church." He saw her jaw clench, but she eased back beside him, focusing on her chili. "A few weeks ago, a restaurateur contacted me about the building. They're interested in taking over the whole building and using it for a restaurant."

She shifted a glance his way. "But I thought it was unsafe. That's what you told me, right?"

"It is. You can't just start moving things around with that particular building. It's going to take a lot of money and effort to fix it. In fact, it doubles the budget and timetable."

"It doesn't make it a very good investment then, right?"

Her reaction certainly wasn't what he'd expected. "But it's saving the building," he offered. "That's good, right?"

She took a bite of her chili and nodded her head.

Would he ever truly understand women? She hated the idea of them tearing it down, but now that he was telling her that they were going to do everything possible to keep it up, she looked as though she could care less.

He sat back with his chili and ate as he watched the fire. No need to dive any deeper into the conversation that obviously was going nowhere.

Picking up the remote, he turned on the TV. The silence between them was suffocating. He searched until he found a football talk show. Well, if she wasn't going to engage him in conversation, he'd watch something that piqued his interest, and forgo the romantic comedy for some other time when he gave a damn about what she was feeling.

ABIGAIL WATCHED HIM STIR HIS CHILI AND BITE DOWN ON HIS spoon. Obviously, her reaction wasn't the one he'd been hoping for. A week ago she'd have been ecstatic to hear the news. She hated to think the church would be torn down. But after Mrs. Winters' comments, she wasn't sure what to tell him. Perhaps she'd only meant not to let him tear it down. That made the most sense in her head. So his news should be good, she thought.

Tomorrow she'd go back to visit Mrs. Winters and ask her. She couldn't let this building tear them apart. It had already been something that caused them pain.

"I'm sorry," she said softly, and she noticed he didn't react. Perhaps he hadn't heard her. "I said I'm sorry." She spoke louder this time.

He clicked the TV off and set his bowl on the table. "I don't get it, Abi. I just can't break through to you." He stood and walked to the bedroom, shutting the door behind him.

Pain ripped through her. It physically sickened her. She lifted her spoon to her lips and noticed how her hands shook. Without taking the bite, she replaced the spoon.

She'd made a mess of things, again. It wasn't worth it. She'd apologize after she cleaned up.

Abigail piled everything back on the tray and carried it to the kitchen. She turned off the slow cooker so that the leftover chili could cool. She rinsed the bowls in the sink and set them to soak as she unloaded the dishwasher.

She heard the TV come on in the living room. Good, she thought. He'd come out. That was a good sign.

The TV grew louder and louder, and she wondered what kind

of point he was trying to make. She wouldn't argue. He had the right to throw a temper tantrum.

She continued to unload the dishwasher, and the TV grew even louder. It was starting to get ridiculous. Then she heard the bedroom door and Carson cursing at the TV.

With the last bowl in her hand, she walked out to see him sitting on the couch, the remote aimed at the TV as if he were trying to turn it off.

It was then she saw the woman behind him kiss the top of his head, just as the TV sound turned off and Abigail dropped the bowl.

Carson turned to her, but all she could do was watch as Mrs. Winters blew her a kiss and faded from sight.

CHAPTER 33

$\mathcal{T}$he damn TV stopped working, but the crash of the bowl to the floor caught Carson's attention. He turned to see Abigail nearly petrified in the kitchen, and the bowl shattered at her feet.

"Abi?" He stood quickly and moved to her, the air chilly around them. "Are you breathing? Answer me," he said as he took her hands and guided her wide stare to him. "Breathe, baby. Breathe. It's just a bowl. The TV must be broken, and damn if the fire isn't..."

"Call Glenn," she said, her voice trembling as she spoke.

The moment she mentioned Glenn's name his chest ached as if she'd pulled his heart from his chest and squeezed the life from it.

Moving her from the glass on the floor, Carson walked Abigail to the kitchen table and helped her sit down. She was a white as a sheet.

"I'll get you something to drink. Some water," he said hoping the small talk would calm her.

"Call Glenn," she repeated. "You have to call..."

At that moment Carson's phone rang on the counter. They both looked at it as it rang.

Finally, he moved toward the counter. Glenn's name was on the ID.

Carson's throat went dry as he pushed the button.

"Hey, Glenn," he answered and heard his voice crack. He watched Abigail's face distort the pain of holding in the tears that pooled in her eyes. She knew what Glenn was saying to him, of that he was certain. A few moments later, they said their good-byes and Carson disconnected the call.

He turned to the counter, bracing himself up with both hands. He could hear her sobs now. Did he have to tell her?

Fighting his own pain, he took a breath. "Mrs. Winters passed about twenty minutes ago."

Carson could hear her sobbing grow heavier now, but he couldn't turn around. He couldn't let go of the damn counter because he didn't trust his own legs beneath him.

When he heard Abigail's breath calm, he turned to watch her dab her eyes with the handkerchief Mrs. Winters had given her.

"She was here, wasn't she?" he asked, not even believing those kinds of words would come from him.

Abigail nodded. "She kissed you goodbye."

Carson closed his eyes, and he could feel the kiss on the back of his head.

"The TV?"

"I think she was trying to get our attention."

Now he moved to her and pulled her from her chair. Wrapping his arms tightly around her, he buried his face in her hair and let the tears fall from his eyes.

This day was inevitable. How many times had he played it out in his mind since they'd become as close as he'd been with her grandson? She was old, and she'd lived a long and full life. It wasn't fair to any of them to be sad. It was selfishness, that was all. The pain was nearly as crippling as when Jeffery died.

"Carson, I'm so sorry," Abigail whispered into his neck.

All he could do was continue to hold her. Love would shield him from the pain, he thought. She would make him calm.

∾

As hard as Carson tried, he couldn't focus at the office. He was a wreck, and so was his mother. Emily had been on the phone with the florist ordering arrangements from the Stone family, and another from Abigail and Carson.

Glenn had called with funeral details. He'd asked for Carson to be a pallbearer along with her other grandsons. Coming from Jeffery's father, he couldn't help but feel the honor of being Jeffery's replacement.

By noon, Carson was spent. He simply couldn't stand to be in his office any longer. After convincing his mother that he was mentally stable, he headed out to his car and began to drive.

He hadn't thought about where he'd go, but as if the car had driven itself, he found himself on the winding roads leading to the apex of Lookout Mountain. He continued until he had driven to the site where they had camped all those years ago—where Jeffery had died.

Was he there too, Carson wondered. If Abigail were with him, would she see him? Why had she seen Mrs. Winters?

Carson parked his car and began to hike toward the picnic table where they'd set up their meek camp that fateful night so many years ago. It had been a long time since he'd been there. The unease of it never settled, no matter how many years had passed.

Around him, the wind blew through the trees which were at the end of their fall color cycle. On the ground dried leaves blew. He could feel Jeffery there, but did he feel him, or was that all part of what was clouding his head? Mrs. Winters told Abigail that she saw him—talked to him. Was that possible?

Carson pressed his fingers to his eyes. Of course, it was possible. Abigail had seen Mrs. Winters kiss him goodbye. So why couldn't he accept that?

He sat there in silence as the cold wind blew around him, and then his skin grew warm. The sun peeked through the sparsely covered branches of the trees, and the breeze grew quiet.

Sitting alone in nature, he realized he wasn't alone at all. Jeffery was there. He could feel him, even though he couldn't see him.

"Jeff?" he asked the open air as if he might just answer. "How do I know if you're really here? I can't see you. But I feel you."

A warm breeze circled him and he could smell the distinct smell of mint flavored chewing tobacco.

Carson burst out into laughter. "Oh my God! You are here."

Now what to say to the man he couldn't see—or the boy he decided.

"I miss you. God, I miss you, my friend." Tears stung his eyes again, and he let the tears build and fall. "I know your grandmother is with you now. I know that you've been waiting for her, but I miss her. It's only been a day and I feel like part of me is missing."

He wiped at the tears that streamed over his cheeks. "I wish you were here to meet Abigail. Your grandmother made that happen." Now he laughed through the tears. "She's everything I didn't know I wanted," he mused. "She's perfect in every way, even the part she hates. See, she can see things like your grandmother could. Though I didn't know that was a skill your grandmother had. I'll have four children with this woman I plan to marry." He chuckled to himself. "I suppose I should name one Jeffery too."

The leaves around him blew from the ground into a cyclone propelled by nothing he could feel around him. He was sure he'd gone absolutely crazy when he thought they resembled the figure of a man before they fell back to the ground.

"You always did love magic tricks," he said wiping his cheeks again. "I'm so glad you showed up today to let me talk to you." He felt the warmth on his cheeks. "I'm going to propose to Abigail when your grandma's funeral is over, and we've begun to move on without her. Your dad is holding up well, though I would guess you know that."

Carson stood from his seat on the bench. "I'll come back. Maybe I can bring Abi, and you can meet her." He smiled at the strange notion that it might be completely different with her there. She could probably see him. "Goodbye, my friend."

The air around him circled the leaves at his feet again, and then it went cold. As he shook off the chill, he realized that Jeffery was gone and the clouds had darkened the sky, except for one spot by the base of the tree. The sun broke through and shone on the ground. From the pile of leaves, he saw something bright catch his eye.

Carson moved to it, kneeling down beneath the tree. He brushed away the leaves, and on the ground was Jeffery's class ring.

His breath caught in his lungs as he looked down at it. Had it been there for the past sixteen years? Had no one found it as they picnicked and played in the area?

Carson gripped it in his hand and held it to his heart. "I'll see that your mother gets this," he said, and the patch of sunlight between the branches of the trees grew dark just like the rest of the sky.

Now instead of tobacco, he could smell the impending snow the forecasters had promised.

CHAPTER 34

"*A*bi, take a break. You're going to make yourself sick running around here like this," Clare scolded her as she counted the cookies on the tray one more time.

Because she didn't know what else to do for the family, Abigail had offered up The Tea Shop for a reception after the funeral. Because it was Mrs. Winters, she wanted everything to be perfect. However, she hadn't slept since Mrs. Winters had waved goodbye to her.

When the bell over the front door chimed, and she jumped as if someone had come from behind a tree with an ax, Clare moved through the kitchen to see who it was. "Stay in here. You're too messed up for a customer to see."

A few moments later Clare and Carson walked through the door of the kitchen together.

Under the wool overcoat, he was dressed in a three-piece suit, was freshly shaven, and smelled of heaven. He certainly was apt to make an impression.

"Are you ready?" he asked, his voice soft and sad.

"I don't know. The shop isn't set up all the way. I keep losing track on my count for these cookies, and..."

Clare gripped her shoulders. "And if you don't get the hell out of my way, it won't be ready at all. Now go. I will have everything set up when you get back."

On any other day, Abigail would argue with her. Today, she felt weak, so she pulled her cousin in and hugged her. "I love you. Thank you."

"I love you, too. Now go."

Carson helped her with her apron when it tangled, and he held her coat so she could slide into it. His car had been cleaned and waxed. It sat, a brilliant shiny black against the newly fallen snow.

"I am absolutely sure Mrs. Winters ordered snow in October just to have her funeral. It's fitting," he said as he opened the car door and Abigail slid in.

"It shimmers in the sunlight," Abigail added.

"Yeah, just like she did."

He shut the door and walked around the car. Shrugging out of the overcoat, he opened the back door and set the coat on the seat. He closed the door and opened the other. A crisp breeze blew into the car as he slid in.

For a moment he sat silently, his hands on the wheel. "I've known this day was coming for years. I don't think you're any better prepared when it gets here though."

Abigail reached for his hand. Again, she saw the cloud of darkness, and she felt the dampness on her skin.

Quickly she pulled back. He was distraught enough, and he didn't seem to notice her reaction.

A moment later Carson pulled away from the curb and headed to the church where they would say their final goodbyes to a woman that meant the world to both of them.

～

THE FUNERAL HAD BEEN WELL ATTENDED, WHICH TOLD CARSON

that the woman who had filled a void in his life had touched many others.

Though he'd been very close to her son Glenn's family most of his life, it was the first time he'd met Jeffery's other cousins, but they all seemed to know him.

It was interesting that Mrs. Winters had loved him as much as everyone said she had. She wasn't his grandmother, but even talking to her own grandchildren, no one would have been the wiser. She was proud of him, and she boasted about how well he did in business and the good he did for the community. Mrs. Winters' daughter even knew all about Abigail, and she'd shared that she was happy to see that they had finally found each other.

After Carson helped carry Mrs. Winters to her final resting place, he took a few minutes to visit Jeffery only a few feet away.

The hand on his shoulder told him that Abigail understood his pain. She stood quietly to his side, but her presence eased the ache in his heart.

"I went up the mountain the other day and talked to him," he said still crouching in front of his headstone. "He was there. I felt him. I smelled him," he said with a chuckle. "At one point I thought I could see him."

"I think you did too."

Carson looked up at her. "You've talked to him?"

She shook her head. "I think Mrs. Winters wanted you and I to have something more in common. She told me so in a dream, but it didn't make any sense to me. But if you saw him, then she's instilled that in you."

Carson stood. "So now I'll see the future?"

She shrugged. "Or you'll see her and Jeffery. You'll only see what you want to see. But your mind is open now."

CARSON TOOK HER HAND AND LACED THEIR FINGERS TOGETHER. "You don't see anything with us, still?"

Abigail shook her head. "I'm glad, actually. I want it all to be fresh and new."

He pulled her to him and pressed a kiss to her forehead. "I love you, Abigail Weston. I can't imagine the pain my heart would be going through if you weren't here. I didn't know how I'd recover from the loss of Jeffery, and Mrs. Winters was there for me. Now you're here while I process my loss of her."

"I'll never leave your side," she promised, even though she could feel the world begin to spin as he held her hand. There was something coming she thought as he broke the connection and turned to one of Jeffery's cousins who stood and began to reminisce with Carson.

How was she supposed to know how to stop whatever inevitable bad was to come his way if she were now alone with her ability? Carson had somehow summonsed Jeffery on his trip to the mountain. Could Abigail summons Mrs. Winters in more than just her dreams? She would have to try because now she was too deep in love with the man to lose him and not know what was coming for them.

∾

AFTER THE FUNERAL, MRS. WINTERS' ENTIRE FAMILY CONVERGED on The Tea Shop. As Clare had promised, she had everything ready and set up as they had planned.

Mrs. Winters' daughter Donna moved to Carson and Abigail as they stood with Jeffery's brother.

"Abigail, this is a lovely place. I've been meaning to come by and see it. My mother talked about it all the time. It looks so different from when she had her linen shop here," she said as she looked around.

"I'm sorry, she had what?" Abigail asked.

Donna smiled as she lifted her teacup to her apricot painted lips. "She never mentioned it? Oh, when my mother and father had first started out, she and her mother opened a linen shop in this very spot. They sold bed and table linens, oh and appliquéd handkerchiefs. That was one of their specialties."

Abigail pulled the handkerchief from her pocket, which Mrs. Winters had given her. "Like this?"

Donna's eyes went wide. "Oh, my goodness. Yes. Where did you get that?"

"Your mother gave it to me the day before she passed. I didn't realize it had such a history. I suppose it should go to you then, or one of your children," Abigail said looking down at the piece of art she held in her hand.

"Not at all. She gave it to you. Oh, Abigail, she thought the world of you. To think you share her space where she loved to come and create. I simply can't believe she didn't tell you about that."

Abigail couldn't believe it either. Was there more than their shared gift that had brought them together?

Donna moved on to talk to other family members, and others moved in to thank her and Clare for inviting them in to celebrate Mrs. Winters' life.

AT THE END OF THE NIGHT, ABIGAIL LAID IN BED CLUTCHING THE handkerchief to her chest. What did it all mean, she wondered, as Carson lay beside her snoring softly. What purpose was there for her to walk in Mrs. Winters' footsteps?

CHAPTER 35

They had both decided to take off the Friday after Mrs. Winters' funeral. A few days to collect themselves was needed.

Abigail left the clean up of the store to Clare, as she was asked to do, and decided to give her own house a thorough cleaning.

Carson had opted to work in his own house for a few hours, but promised he'd be back to sleep in her arms.

Abigail kept the handkerchief she'd been given in the front pocket of her jeans. There was some odd comfort in having it with her.

When she'd gone to bed the night before, she'd tried to summons Mrs. Winters to her dreams, but she hadn't come. There were just too many unanswered questions. If she could just have one more conversation with her, maybe she could put to rest the uncertainties she was feeling.

Abigail cleaned the house from top to bottom, never once turning on the TV or radio for noise. Solitude was what she'd needed to lift her spirits. Carson, however, wasn't as lifted when he returned.

BERNADETTE MARIE

Along with a huge knot on the side of his head where a board had fallen, his attitude was sour.

He kicked off his dusty shoes next to the door, where she'd mopped, threw his jacket on the fluffed and vacuumed sofa, and he rattled the entire kitchen when he yanked open the refrigerator door to pull out a beer. After he tossed the cap to the beer on the wiped down counter, he chugged back the beer until he'd nearly downed half of it.

"In a mood?" Abigail asked after having witnessed his entrance.

"You could say that," he said slamming the door to the refrigerator.

"Anything I can do to help you through it before it sours my mood too."

When he lifted his eyes to hers, they seemed apologetic, but the words never surfaced.

"Katie Meadows."

She felt her spine straighten and her jaw clench. "You're bringing her up just to piss me off?"

"Nope. I'm bringing her up because she is Ellie Winters' great niece."

Abigail sat down in the nearest chair because her knees had gone weak. "How did you find that out?"

"Donna called me before I came here. The world is a small place," he said taking another pull from his beer. "Donna mentioned your tea shop to another relative who was from Missouri. Enough talking and enough plugging your name into Google, and voila!" He ran his hand over his face and let out a breath.

"I didn't kill Katie Meadows," she said sternly and was surprised when his eyes moved to meet hers, and she saw the disappointment in them.

"Do you think that's why I'm upset about this? You think I still think you killed her?"

Abigail gathered her thoughts. "No. I sincerely think you know better. But I can't read this situation."

Carson set his beer on the table, took Abigail's hand, and pulled her to her feet. "Somehow I think Mrs. Winters used you to find Katie. You said you saw her in your dream in the river."

"Right."

"Just like I think she brought you here, sent you to that building to put your tea shop in, and she brought us together."

"Why me?"

"Why not you?" He ran his hand over her hair. "Donna also said that Mrs. Winters found a young boy once who had been lost. He didn't die, but he was close. People thought Mrs. Winters was some kind of freak of nature for years. But when her gift led her to her husband, she fell in love in a moment, because she knew he was the right one."

"So why are you so upset?" Abigail asked, raising her hands to Carson's chest.

"Because I think you are here to follow her path, and I think we're messing it up."

"I don't understand."

Carson took her hand again and led her to the living room. They sat down on the sofa, their hands still in one another's.

"Mrs. Winters met her husband and married him right away. They lived long and happy lives with their four children. Two sons and two daughters."

Abigail's heart began to race. "You think there is some legacy I'm upholding? I'm not related to her."

"No, but you're cut from the same cloth, if you will. Maybe because of your gift you're connected—like family."

"What does that have to do with me and you then? You're not related to her. I'm not related to her. How did this come to be?"

"I don't know. Maybe you were destined for Jeffery, and I got in the way."

Abigail searched his eyes to see if he believed that. "Really?"

Finally, his shoulders dropped, and he smiled. "No. Maybe she just knew you were a good person and she wanted the very best for me."

Abigail moved in and rested her head on his shoulder, and he held on to her tightly.

"But it did make me decide to do something I've been waiting for."

She sat back and looked into his kind and loving eyes. "What's that?"

Carson stood and pulled his jacket from the back of the sofa. He reached into his pocket and pulled out a box.

"I've had this in my desk drawer for the past week. The only person I've shown it to is my mother." Carson flipped the box open and revealed the diamond he'd bought for her.

"Carson," her voice shook, and tears pooled in her eyes. "What are you doing?"

He slid off the sofa, and onto one knee. "I'm asking you to marry me. Let's start our own future. I know it's only been just over a month since we happened into each other's lives, but I can't think of any reason not to stay in each other's lives. I love you, Abi. Will you be my wife?"

Abigail slid to the floor next to him. She held out her hand, and he slid the ring on her finger. "I'm scared to death."

Carson let out a chuckle. "Me too. To be honest, until the day I met you, I didn't think I'd ever do this."

"I didn't think anyone would accept me enough to do it either."

"Well, we were both wrong. Abigail, will you marry me?"

She looked down at her finger and back up at his misted eyes. How could she possibly love someone as much as she loved him?

"I would be honored to be your wife."

Carson pulled her to him, and they held each other, on their knees on the living room floor.

"I'm going to make a million mistakes," he promised.

"And if only I could read you, I'd know they were coming."

They both laughed as they held each other, anticipating what was to come for them.

CHAPTER 36

*B*eing engaged seemed to be the perfect magic to getting things done. Carson had moved all of his essentials into Abigail's house. They'd discussed it at length. They would finish Carson's house and rent it. When the time came that Abigail's house became too small, they'd rent it too and buy something bigger.

It wasn't until Carson had gone to lunch with Glenn that he knew exactly where they would live when they got married.

After work on a snowy evening before Thanksgiving, Carson took his bride-to-be to dinner. She and his mother had been busy with wedding planning, and she led the conversation. If she quizzed him, he was dead meat because he hadn't heard a word she'd said. His mind was preoccupied with his conversation with Glenn.

After dinner, as Abigail was still talking about wedding venues and colors, he started toward Genesee—then she began to pay attention.

"Where are you going?" she asked as she looked out the window.

"I want to show you something."

"You're heading to Mrs. Winters' house, aren't you?"

Carson chuckled and reached for her hand. "I can't pull anything over on you, can I?"

"More than most people. Why are you going to her house?"

"Glenn said it's finished, remodeled, and looks fantastic. He gave me the key so I could check it out. Is this okay?" He hadn't thought about what she might see in the house that he couldn't see.

"I think that sounds wonderful. I can't wait to see what they've done."

Relieved, he relaxed a bit. "Glenn said it had more water damage than fire damage."

"I never did hear what caused the fire."

"A candle," he said, and he heard the sadness of it. "She'd forgotten it, and it nearly cost her her life. She seemed sharp till the end, but it was the little things like that which could have hurt her or someone else."

The porch lights shimmered as they pulled up. Though the damage had been primarily to the back of the house, no one would ever have known there had been a fire by driving up to the front, Carson thought as he parked the car in the driveway.

As he climbed out, so did Abigail. Hand in hand they walked to the front door. Carson slid in the key that Glenn had given him, and they walked into the house together.

The smell of fresh paint and wood filled his nose. It had become one of his more favorite scents.

Carson began to turn on lights in the now empty house.

Abigail gave his hand a squeeze. "It looks fantastic."

"They did a real nice job."

They walked to the kitchen, where the majority of the work had been done. It was a newly renovated kitchen with the newest appliances and a beautiful hardwood floor.

Abigail ran her hand over the countertops. "Clare would be envious of this kitchen."

"What about you? You don't like the kitchen?"

She glanced up at him. "It's a lovely kitchen."

"We have the key. We could cook something here," he offered and her brows drew inward.

"Why would I cook in someone else's house?"

He eased her into his arms. "Glenn offered me the house. It's the perfect size for four kids," he explained with a smile he could feel rising from his chest.

"Here? Us?"

He nodded. "Glenn thought it would be a good home for us if we wanted to buy it from the family. He let me have the key so we could feel it out. What do you think?"

"Oh, Carson, I don't know." She looked around hesitantly. "This is a lot to think about."

"We can rent out both of our houses and that will help cover the mortgage. Glenn is willing to cut us a fantastic deal."

ABIGAIL STEPPED BACK FROM HIM AND FOLDED HER ARMS AROUND herself. She circled the kitchen and walked to the family room where she stood looking at the walls. Ellie Winters' family photos had once hung there. Her children had played on the floor and in the backyard.

She closed her eyes and took a few deep breaths. Why couldn't she feel her in the house? She'd fully expected to.

Was that a sign that she'd passed over to be with Jeffery and her husband? Was she truly at peace?

Abigail was sure that if Mrs. Winters didn't agree with her son's offer, she'd let them know about it.

"Show me the rest of the house," she said and noticed the smile widen on Carson's mouth.

Carson took her through the house explaining all the rooms as he'd remembered them from when Jeffery had taken him through many times when they were younger. As an adult, he never went further than the kitchen or living room, but he had his own stories of the house as a child.

Abigail was relieved to find absolute calm when they stood in Mrs. Winters' bedroom. It was just a newly remodeled house, she realized, but one that came with happy memories for her fiancé.

"This is what you want to do? You want to live here?" she asked as she turned to Carson.

"I do. But only if you want to too. We're partners now."

Abigail looked around the room taking it all in. She then moved to Carson and wrapped her arms around his neck. "I think this would be a lovely place to start our life together."

Carson planted a kiss on her that nearly buckled her knees. "That makes me happy," he said as he held her tightly.

"It makes me happy, too."

~

THEY'D MANAGED FOLDING TABLES AND CHAIRS INTO THE HOUSE before both families converged on it for Thanksgiving. Carson's father had carried in a brand new television, a housewarming gift, he told them. With help from Abigail's father, they managed to get a football game to come through.

Abigail listened as her mother and Patricia sat at one of the card tables and made more wedding plans. It was all happening, and both of their families were involved.

After Abigail left Missouri, she wasn't sure she'd ever had a sense of family or community again. Thankfully she had it now. She could never have guessed that her move would change her life as much as it had.

Carson stepped up behind her and wrapped his arms around her waist. "They're all getting along."

"Did you expect them not to?"

He chuckled. "You hear horror stories. Perhaps we'll never

have that. We won't have to slip from one dinner to attend the other. Neither of us will start a drinking habit before a holiday."

Abigail elbowed him in the gut as she laughed. "Imagine what those two will be like when they have a grandchild." She nodded in the direction of their mothers.

"They'll be two giddy old women."

"They're not old," she scolded.

"They will be in time, and they'll spoil our kids rotten."

"That's their job, right?"

He placed a kiss on her head. "I wouldn't want it any other way."

There was a pang of sadness that filled her as she watched their families. "I'm sorry that Mrs. Winters isn't here for all of this. It makes me sad that she won't see our wedding or meet our children."

Carson turned her to face him. "I guarantee that she and your grandmother are picking out our children." He narrowed his gaze at her. "You weren't a troublemaker were you?"

"Me? Are you kidding?"

"I had to ask. We will be fifty percent okay then."

"Why fifty?"

"I was a troublemaker," he said as he winked and she pressed her cheek to his chest. As sorry as she was that Mrs. Winters wasn't around, she was forever grateful that she'd intervened. Without her, Abigail was sure she would never be this happy.

CHAPTER 37

*T*hanksgiving quickly gave way to the Christmas season. Though Clare and Abigail had set up a few Christmas items before Thanksgiving, Abigail wanted to wait until the season was in full swing before completely decorating.

They spent the Sunday after Thanksgiving setting up Christmas trees and adorning the windows with greenery. She couldn't have imagined that her fiancé would whistle Christmas tunes the entire day, but he had.

Patricia had stopped by as well, hoping to lend a hand. Abigail was sure she had many more plans than she'd offered, but that was one sign she would be a gracious mother-in-law, she thought.

When Clare and Patricia had left, and the sun had tucked itself away, Abigail and Carson sat in the dark tea shop having a cup of peppermint tea and watching the lights twinkle around them.

"I can imagine Mrs. Winters' store here," she said as she looked around. "The walls lined with shelves with fabrics. Displays of beautifully adorned handkerchiefs, or personalized pillowcases."

"She's showed that to you?"

Abigail shook her head. "No. She hasn't appeared or visited in my sleep," she confirmed. "I have to assume she moved on to the other side and is content."

Carson reached his hand across the table and took hers. "And you still can't read me, huh?"

"Nope. I assume it's your stubborn streak," she joked as she gave his hand a squeeze.

"And not yours?"

She shrugged. "Maybe."

Carson turned in his seat to face her. "I was thinking, I know we're not getting married until February, but don't you think we should move into the house now?"

The very thought should have enticed her, she thought. She couldn't wait to move into the house. So, why couldn't she give him an answer?

They'd been living together since the beginning, she considered. They planned to live together for the rest of their lives. Why should waiting until February make it better?

She didn't have an answer for that. But something didn't sit right with it. All she could assume was that she was getting in her own way. She did that enough, she knew.

Besides, if they moved now, they could rent out her house. Perhaps, if they got tenants in soon enough, they could buy new furniture, new decorations, or even extend their honeymoon.

She smiled at her handsome fiancé. "I think you're right. I think it would be a good idea." Once she saw the smile cross his lips, she realized it had been the right decision. After all, she had been collecting an overabundance of Christmas decorations for her own house, which now she could put in her new house.

Suddenly the thought of moving into Mrs. Winters' house made her giddy with anticipation. Her grandmother used to love Christmas trees. She had one in nearly every room in her house. Abigail began to mentally count the rooms in the new house.

Carson chuckled. "What are you doing?"

"I was just thinking about how many Christmas trees I needed."

"How many? Don't you only need one Christmas tree? Who needs more than one Christmas tree?"

"I do," she said matter-of-factly. "I have a big, beautiful, new house. I want to decorate it until it sparkles. I want a Christmas tree in every room. I want people to see it from the highway it's so bright."

Carson stood and pulled her to her feet. He kept her hand in his and placed his other hand on her waist. He swayed as if he heard music in his mind, she thought.

The store lights twinkled around them, and she noticed that had to begun to snow outside. It was magic.

"A Christmas tree in every room? People will remember that," he said as he pressed his cheek to hers.

CARSON MADE THE ARRANGEMENTS FOR THE MOVE. CONSTRUCTION seemed to drop off on most projects during the holidays. On the other hand, Abigail was working more hours than usual. He figured since it had been his idea to move into the house before Christmas, he needed to be the one to make most of the plans. Abigail hadn't seemed to argue about that. She was more than happy to leave the packing and moving to someone else. They spent their evenings unpacking and organizing their house. And, in every room, Abigail made sure there was a little bit of Christmas cheer.

CARSON HAD MET WITH THE PRIVATE CONTRACTOR ABOUT WORK AT his house. It was time to get the remodel done. Emily had a cousin who was moving to the area and wanted to rent a house.

He figured if he could get the house done in time, he'd have it rented right away. They already had a renter for Abigail's house, and that had seemed to help ease her into their new home.

As he sat back in his office chair and rested his hands behind his head, he watched as his mother walked through the door carrying a large box. Quickly, he moved to her and helped her ease the box down on his conference table.

"What is this?" he asked as she dusted off her hands.

"Christmas decorations."

"You already decorated the office. What else are you going to put up?"

She swatted a hand at him and smiled. "Oh, these are for your new house, darling. Your wife-to-be said she wanted to decorate every room."

"Yes, she did. So why are you bringing the decorations to my office?"

The smile on his mother's face lightened. "These are your Christmas decorations. The ones you've made throughout the years. Your Christmas stocking is in here. And an assortment of handmade cards that you gave me too."

"Are you kidding me? Why do you have all of this?" he asked as he opened the box.

"These are the kinds of things you keep, Carson. Abigail is going to think they are wonderful."

He shook his head as he pulled out a monstrosity made of popsicle sticks and glitter. "You think she's going to appreciate this? I don't even know what it is."

"It's a star. And yes, I think she's going to adore them."

"If I made all of this for you, why are you giving it away?"

"Because I've enjoyed it for all these years. Now it's time for your own family to enjoy it."

He tucked away the star and closed the box. There was a hint of a tear in her eye when she mentioned his own family. He supposed it was good to know that she was ready for him to move on, get married, and start a family of his own.

They were moving in the right direction, he decided. Abigail would be his wife by February. And maybe they could begin on that family. The thought made him chuckle to himself. He already knew they would have a family, a big family.

He wondered if Abigail ever hated the waiting. After all, once you knew the future, how was it possible to wait for it? He found it made him very anxious. He couldn't wait to see the faces of his four children.

His mother moved about the office as if she were right at home. She dusted off a few items, straightened the chair, and rearranged the periodicals on the counter. What would she think if he told her what he knew? Would it drive her as mad as it was driving him? Probably.

It was better to let her wait. As for him, time couldn't go fast enough.

CHAPTER 38

As he had during the weeks leading up to Christmas, Carson left his office and started toward the tea shop. He'd had no idea that holiday high tea was such an event. Abigail and Clare had been nonstop busy for nearly three weeks. His mother had even stopped in a few days to help them during their busiest times.

He never imagined that he would be a dishwasher, but that's what he had turned into. Every night after work, he headed to the store to help them clean up.

Tonight, however, he needed to stop by the Ford Street church project first. The crews were beginning to work on the stability of the building. It was going to be a long and tedious task, but it would be worth it.

Work at the site had stopped by the time he got there. All the better, he thought, as there was no one there to ask too many questions.

Carson parked his car and stepped out onto the cold frozen ground. He would walk the perimeter and just see what work had been done. He knew better than to go inside at this point, leaving that to the professionals.

He could see that in the lower level, new supports were being brought in. Smaller concrete mixers were chained to one another to keep them safely where they were. A generator hung from a front loader.

Carson checked all the openings to the gate and made sure they were secure as well. The last thing he wanted was for anyone to wander inside.

As he checked the final lock, a cold wind blew through the construction site. His muscles froze as he tried to wrap his coat around him tighter. All the while, he swore he could smell roses.

When the wind died down, he hurried back to his car. He laughed to himself as he started the engine and waited for the heater to kick in.

It was December, snowing, and freezing, how in the world did he think he'd smelled roses?

From the construction site, Carson headed straight to the tea shop. There was no surprise that it was nearing seven o'clock, and the entire place was still full of customers.

He noticed as he walked through the door that not all of the customers were dining on tea. Many of them were looking at the holiday gifts that Abigail and Clare had brought in. However, there was a new display near the cash register he noticed. It was full of adorned handkerchiefs and linens. These looked much different than the ones his mother had purchased that Abigail's mother had made.

Abigail walked from the kitchen, her hands each filled with plates of decadent treats. She smiled at Carson as she walked to the table and sat down plates. He heard her explain each delicacy to the delighted women before she left them.

Carson went straight back to the kitchen and hung up his coat. As he passed Clare, who was making another plate of sandwiches, he kissed her on the cheek. "Is this what you expected at Christmas time?"

"This is what I dreamed of." She smiled widely.

Carson picked up the extra apron that hung on the hook. He tied it around his waist and went straight to the sink. Abigail had been very specific as to how to wash the dishes. Some of the cups were over one hundred years old, and he had to admit he was scared to death to break one.

Abigail fluttered her way through the kitchen, and he noted the smile on her face. She was in her element. She loved the people, the atmosphere, and he'd come to learn that she absolutely loved Christmas.

"Thank you for coming to help. They did a write up on the store in the Golden paper. Did you see it? We've been slammed because of it. The phone has been ringing off the hook," she said as she filled a container with cream. "I had someone call and ask how late we were open. I wasn't quite sure what to say. We're already open longer than usual."

Clare laughed. "She's a little excited," she said to Carson.

"It brings out the pink in her cheeks," he noted.

Abigail moved from the refrigerator to the sink, carrying the creamer in her hand. "I love this time year. And did you see our new display?"

"I did. Where did you get the linens?"

"Donna. They found them in Mrs. Winters' things. They all took what they wanted and kept some for future generations. But she said they have boxes and boxes of it. She thought it belonged here where it was to begin with. I've already sold five or six pieces."

"I'm proud of you. Kiss me and get back to work," he instructed.

Abigail moved to him, rising on her tiptoes. She moved in and pressed a kiss to his lips. He first heard the creamer drop to the floor and the container shatter, right before he heard the breaking of the Prussian cup that he dropped in the sink. It was all a blur as he watched Abigail fall backward and he reached for her.

They both went to the ground, but somehow he managed to get himself underneath her so she didn't hit her head.

"Abi! Abigail, are you okay?"

Her eyelashes fluttered as she tried to open her eyes. "I'm sorry."

"Don't you be sorry. Just lay here a minute."

Clare hurried to them, a glass of water in her hand. "I hate when you do that. You scare the hell out of me."

Carson watched as she came to just enough to sip the water. He would've worried that something was wrong with her, but he'd seen her do this before. As she became more steady, she sat up on her own.

Color began to fill her cheeks and tears her eyes.

He brushed a finger over her cheek as the first tear fell. "Don't cry. You're okay. Do you feel okay?"

She nodded.

He realized, at that moment, he wasn't touching her. He couldn't help but reach out and pressed his fingers to her arm.

Again, he watched her eyes nearly rolled back all the way her head as she fell back into his arms.

Clare moved in quickly. "What the hell is with her?"

"Here. You need to move in and hold her."

He and Clare exchanged positions. The moment that Abigail was fully in Clare's arms, her consciousness returned.

Clare looked at the Carson and a line formed between her brows. "What's going on?"

"I think she had a premonition. I think it was about me, or brought on by me."

They both turn the focus back to Abigail who stared at them. "It was when I kissed you. But there's nothing there. Everything just went black." Abigail brushed the hair from her eyes. "This is a mess. We need to get this cleaned up," she said as she looked up at Carson. "And did you break a Prussian cup?"

Carson held his hands up in surrender. "I will buy you a thousand antique Prussian cups if I never have to see you do that again."

He watched helplessly as Clare helped Abigail to her feet, and then both women cleaned up the cream. Managing to clean out the sink, he threw away the shards of the antique cup.

When he looked up, Abigail stood next to him with a sad look on her face. "I'm sorry."

"I'm not sure what you're apologizing for. You have nothing to be sorry for."

She only nodded and went back to work.

Carson watched as she walked back out to the dining room as if nothing had happened. Inside, his gut twisted. This was what she had feared all along, wasn't it? How could they possibly have a physical relationship if she couldn't touch him?

And why had everything just gone black, he wondered? What did that signify? Was he in danger, or was she?

CHAPTER 39

*I*t was past one in the morning when Carson stumbled out of the bedroom and into the living room. Abigail sat on the sofa, an old quilt wrapped around her and the gas fireplace burning.

"Why are you out here?" he asked, but he knew the answer.

She hadn't come near him the rest of the evening since she'd blacked out in the kitchen. There was no doubt she had the same concerns he had. Would they ever be able to touch again?

"I can't sleep," she said. "I didn't want to wake you."

"You should have," he offered as he moved toward the sofa and noticed she curled up more as he sat down on the other end. "We have to deal with this, Abi. We can't go through our lives not touching."

"That's the problem now, isn't it? If I can't touch you then our fate, our future, is gone. You don't deserve this. You don't."

And that was the first thing that made sense to him. "You can't worry about me. What about you?" Carson fought off the urge to move closer. "Our future is solid. I'm not going anywhere, and neither are you. So this happened. And it will probably happen again. I think we need to face it."

"I don't know that I want to."

"We have to." Now he did move closer, and he pushed away the anger that surfaced as she drew her knees in even closer to her chest. "Abi, touch me."

She shook her head. "No. What if I black out again? What if I don't come to again?"

Carson eased back slightly. He hadn't thought of that. Could something pull her in from the other side and keep her there? This was all beyond anything he'd ever comprehended.

"Let's just start with what happened at the store. I kissed you and then what?"

She took in a deep breath and considered. "You kissed me, and everything went dark. The air swirled around me, well in my head I guess. It was as if it was dusty. I remember not being able to breathe because of the dust."

"But it was just black? You couldn't make out a structure or anything?"

She shook her head. As she lifted her eyes back to his, her shoulders pushed back, and her eyes went wide as if she'd seen something.

"What? What's going on?"

"There was a man," she said as she tossed off the quilt and rose to her feet.

"Where?" He held out his arm as if to stop her from walking any further, careful not to touch her. "Stay here, I'll…"

"No. He's gone." She eased back. "He was here. There," she offered as she pointed behind him.

Carson settled his breath and tried to wrap his head around what she was saying. "A ghost?"

"Yes. Just like when Mrs. Winters kissed you goodbye. He was right there." She pointed again.

A chill ran down his spine. "Who was it?"

"I don't know," she said and then her eyes went wide again. "I think it was Mr. Winters."

"Would you know him if you saw him again?"

Abigail nodded.

Carson went to the room adjacent to their bedroom, which he'd set up as a home office. He retrieved his computer and hurried back to the living room.

Abigail had folded the quilt and neatly set it on the end of the sofa. Carson sat down where he had before, resting his laptop on his knees. As he searched online for a photo of Edward Winters the third, as he remembered from his headstone, Abigail paced around the room.

"Got it," he said as he set the computer on the coffee table and waited for her to sit next to him.

Abigail eased down, careful not to touch him, he noted. "This is him?" she asked as she picked up the computer.

"Yeah. It's a photo from Glenn's Facebook page. Is that the man you saw?"

Abigail shook her head. "No."

Carson sat back on the sofa and let out a breath. "I wonder who you saw, and why is he in our house?"

She set the computer back on the table. "How did Mr. Winters die?"

"Mine collapsed on him, I think." He picked back up the computer and searched for the information. "Here. 1988 there were two victims who died in a mine accident when it collapsed on them." He read the article. "Justice Mason, 58, and Edward Winters, 53."

"She was a widow all those years?"

"I guess she was. I didn't realize that. I knew I'd never met Jeffery's grandfather. I guess as a kid you figure that's normal."

"Were they mining?"

Carson continued to read the article. "No, they were hunting. It says the two men were caught in the mine when it collapsed after pulling out a child who had fallen into the mine. Xavier Montoya, six, had wandered from his family's campsite. After falling into the mine, he was rescued by two hunters who had passed by. The men were able to get him out of the mine, and his family was there to pull him up. However, the mine collapsed around the hunters before they could escape."

Abigail's hand moved to her mouth, and he heard the sob escape. It ached not to pull her into his arms and console her.

"Look up Justice Mason. Did you know him?"

He shook his head. "No. I'll look."

"I'll make some coffee. I don't see us getting any sleep now."

Carson nodded and began to plug in the names they were learning. He went to his office for a notepad and felt the cold hover over him. Keeping himself steady, he could only assume that the man Abigail had seen was still with them. What did he want?

He could hear her in the kitchen as he went back to his computer.

Justice Mason was from Saint Louis, Missouri, which seemed to set off an alarm in Carson's brain. A little more digging, he found that in fact he was related to Ellie Winters. He was her brother-in-law.

Carson sat back and closed his eyes. What a horrible trauma for her to have gone through. In one moment she lost her husband and her sister lost hers. Then years later they would lose Jeffery too. How had the woman stayed so kind he wondered.

Abigail walked from the kitchen with two cups of coffee on the silver tray she'd had at her own house. There were also biscotti on a small plate.

"Thanks," he said as she stepped back and let him pick up his cup.

"Did you find anything."

"Justice Mason was Mrs. Winters brother-in-law."

Her eyes had gone wide as she sat down on the other end of the sofa. "That's so sad."

"The only photo I can find of all of them was on Donna's

Facebook page. It looks like it might be a wedding photo of Mr. and Mrs. Winters."

He turned the computer to face her. "That's him," she said pointing to the screen. "The man on the left."

"That's Justice Mason."

"The little girl. Who is that?"

Carson turned the computer to face him as he searched the notes Donna had made on the photo. The girl Abigail had referred to was perhaps two-years-old, and it appeared that she was the flower girl for the wedding.

"All it says is Larissa."

Abigail stood and walked to the fire. He watched as she stared down at it. "He's back. He's standing right next to you."

Carson turned his head, but he saw no one there, though he could feel the air had chilled around him again.

"Can you talk to him?"

She shook her head. "I can't hear him." She stood by the fire for another moment before turning around. She looked past Carson, and he had to assume she was looking right at the man. "Are you Justice?" she asked, and he could hear the tremor in her voice.

Carson waited for a reaction.

"He nodded."

"Ask him if he knows Larissa."

"Do you know Larissa?" she asked and waited. "He nodded again. Now he's holding his arms like he's holding a baby."

Abigail exchanged glances with Carson then looked past him again. "Larissa is your daughter?" she asked the man and then waited. "He nodded again."

He wasn't sure where this would all lead or why the man had decided to visit them in the middle of the night, but he'd admit to her later that he was fascinated by it all.

Abigail moved back to the sofa and turned the computer. She studied the photo, and he watched as her mouth opened and she looked back up, beyond him. "Larissa. She married and had a little girl?"

Carson sat in the silence and watched the conversation his fiancée was having to empty air.

"What did he say?"

"Yes."

"How do you know that? Who is his granddaughter?"

Abigail's eyes locked on his. He could see the tears form and fall over her cheeks. "Katie Meadows."

CHAPTER 40

*A*bigail's hands shook as she sat on the sofa next to Carson. When she saw him reach for her, she quickly stood and stepped away. He couldn't touch her. Not now.

The man, whom she now knew as Justice Mason, Katie Meadows grandfather, had disappeared as quietly as he'd come in. The fire went on to heat the house, and the chill disappeared.

"I should get ready for work and go in early. I need to do something. I need to..."

Carson stood and moved toward her, stopping only inches away. "You need to calm down. You're not going to work today."

Abigail fisted her hands on her hips. "I most certainly am. It's not like your business where you can come and go as you please. I won't do that to Clare."

"Clare will be fine. I'm going to call my mother in a bit and ask her to go in for you. She's been working with you. She knows the drill." He took one step closer and stopped. "I'm not going to let my fiancée fall apart like this. We need some answers, and we need them now."

"I don't have any."

"No, so we're going to get some." He turned and headed

toward the kitchen before stopping and looking over his shoulder. "C'mon. Sit at the table while I make some toast. Coffee before four A.M. Makes me a bit jittery."

He disappeared into the kitchen while she stood alone in the living room contemplating what had happened that night.

In the past, she'd felt her grandmother around her, but she'd never seen her. Katie Meadows came to her in a dream, though it wasn't her coming through. It had been a vision of where they'd find her. The fire in the very house where she stood had come to her in a vision. She'd never been visited before with her eyes open until Mrs. Winters had come to say goodbye.

Was this a new skill? Was she going to be awakened by ghosts all the time now? She certainly hoped not. All she wanted was something normal, but there was a deep seeded feeling that kept her from thinking she'd have that. Why had she blacked out when Carson had kissed her? Was it that Justice was trying to come through at the same time? That had to be it, right? There was a long line of coincidences. However, she also felt as though her soul connected with that of Ellie Winters, and more than just by chance.

She knew her family wasn't related to Katie Meadows' family. She'd long ago researched that trying to find answers as to why she'd been the one to have the vision. Was it possible to be connected with another soul without a genetic attachment?

"Are you coming?" Carson called from the kitchen.

Abigail started toward him, and panic rose in her chest. She didn't feel as though Justice's visit was a thank you of sorts. She still felt as though there was a warning in everything that had happened.

Carson stood at the counter putting bread into the toaster. "How many slices do you want?"

"Kiss me," she blurted out, and he turned around. "Kiss me right now."

"Abi, what's going on?"

too much to ask?" She swiftly moved toward him, but his hands came up in surrender.

"Is it too much to ask?" She swiftly moved toward him, but his hands came up in surrender.

"Slow down."

Anger began to build inside of her. "I want to see it again. I need to know what was coming through. Kiss me."

Carson put down his hands. "We need some ground rules." He turned and canceled the toaster and then threw the pieces of bread into the trash. "I saw what happened to you at the store. I don't want to see that again."

"I can't guarantee that."

"I know." He leaned back against the counter and folded his arms in front of him as if to keep his hands from reaching for her. "If I kiss you and it happens again, how long do I let it go? I'm the only one here. I can't pass you off as I did with Clare."

She had to agree that sounded frightful. "If I go under like that hold me for a few minutes."

"When do I call for help?"

"I don't know. I just blacked out. It's not like I stop breathing or anything."

He nodded in agreement slowly. "It reminds me of watching Poltergeist. I don't know if you're going to slip away from me or someone is going to take you over. I'm scared."

"I have to know. Why did I see that before Justice Mason visited me? Was I seeing them in the mine? Was that all?"

"You think if you go under longer you'll get answers?"

"I don't know. All I know is I need to try. I can't go the rest of my life without touching you."

"God, I'm glad to hear that." Carson stood up and moved to her. "Maybe we should sit on the floor, so you don't fall."

Abigail smiled. "That's wise."

"I'm calling 9-1-1 if you don't come back out fast enough."

"Fair enough. However, you have to tell them about the visions and the spirit that visited us tonight. At least if they lock us away maybe, they'll keep us together."

239

He chuckled. "At least you're gaining a sense of humor."

They both eased to the floor without touching one another.

"How are we going to do this?"

"Sit against the counter," she instructed, and he followed. Then she moved in close, still without touching him. "I'm going to kiss you, then if I black out, you can ease me down."

"I still don't like this," he said one more time.

"I need this."

Abigail moved in slowly, breathing in courage as she cupped Carson's face with her hands and leaned in to press her lips to his.

At first, she felt nothing but the warm sensation of the kiss, but a moment later her head began to spin, just as it had before.

She felt Carson's hands come to her sides, his lips still pressed against hers, but darkness was coming quickly.

His fingers dug into her sides now, and she wasn't sure if they were still kissing or if she'd fallen into his arms. All she knew was she was surrounded by cold darkness and it was hard to breathe.

Knowing that she'd taken herself into the dark, she forced herself to be aware of it. It was cold and damp. The air was dusty, and it clogged her lungs. She felt herself cough, but there was no sound.

Was she in the mine with Justice and Edward? Was she seeing what they went through? If so, that had to serve some purpose.

No, she wasn't in a mine. There was light. It was very dim, but there was light. Perhaps a door?

She hadn't heard herself cough, but she heard the rattling noise around her as if the walls were shaking.

Abigail looked around, and she saw a beam falling toward her, but it never hit. Someone else screamed, and she felt the dust kick up around them. Who was there with her? What was this showing her?

A moment later she felt her skin warm, and the air cleared. Where was she going now, she wondered? The warmth of

Carson's mouth on hers brought her back to her senses, and his touch gently caressed her skin.

When she eased back, she looked into his smiling face.

"Thank goodness you didn't black out," he said. "I know it hasn't even been a day, but I was dying not kissing you."

Abigail sat back on her heels. "You were kissing me?"

Worry clouded his eyes now. "Yes. It was a nice long kiss. You held my face and kissed me."

"Right."

"You don't remember?"

She pushed a smile to her lips. "I remember. I just expected to feel something out of the ordinary. But I agree with you, and I'd rather have nice kisses."

"Maybe Justice was here just to thank you."

Abigail nodded and rose to her feet. She held out her hand to help him up. There was nothing but warmth when she touched him, and he stood up.

"I'm going to make more toast and then call my mom. We're still taking the day off," he said as he pulled another two slices of bread from the bag and dropped them in the toaster.

"I think that sounds nice. I'm going to go take a shower."

She walked from the kitchen, and when she was securely out of sight, she fell against the wall in the hallway.

How was it he didn't know what she'd been through? Hadn't she reacted at all?

Someone else needed her help. She was sure of that. Only she didn't know who. Did it have something to do with Justice Mason or Katie Meadows? Had he only come to say thank you?

Abigail pressed her hand to her chest and felt the rapid beat of her heart. She had to figure it out soon. She wasn't sure how much more of this she could take.

CHAPTER 41

hey'd taken the day off and managed the calm they'd been looking for. Though Carson was sure to take it easy, he also made sure he touched Abigail often, both keeping close tabs on her reaction and letting her know how much he loved her.

When the sun peeked out around noon, they took a walk down the street and back again, holding hands. They made a batch of apple cider and sat by the twinkling lights of the Christmas tree as they listened to classic Christmas music. Carson thought it was as magical as it could get.

"I know we have a week left, but sitting here like this, I want to give you one of your presents."

"One of them?"

He laughed that she seemed surprised. He'd known better than to put them all under the tree. Carson suspected she was a present shaker. "Christmas morning you'll have a bounty."

She glanced toward the growing number of gifts under the tree which had been left by his mother and others had been coming in the mail from her family.

"Where is it?"

Carson chuckled. "I thought you'd scold me for that. You're one of those antsy kids that had an alarm set on Christmas morning hoping you catch Santa aren't you?"

She shook her head. "Never wanted to catch him. That would ruin the magic. But I did make them all get up at five in the morning to open gifts."

"Your mother stood for that?"

"No. We all got one, and then we had to wait until the sun was up and we'd eaten breakfast."

"That sounds more like it." Carson stood from his seat on the floor and walked to his office. When he returned, his bride-to-be was seated on her heels like an anxious child.

"What is it?" She bounced up and down, and it brought out a laugh from him.

He held out the envelope he'd collected from his desk. "God, I can't wait to see you open all your gifts for Christmas. You're making me a bit giddy."

"Give it," she took the envelope and opened it slowly.

"What's taking you so long?"

"There is an art to getting the best reaction from a gift. Envelopes make me leery though. Usually, you have to wait for what's inside an envelope. It's usually a promissory note of sorts."

"You never cease to amaze me."

He watched as she pulled out the blue legal form he'd placed in the envelope only the day before. He'd wanted to give it to her when they closed up the tea shop the night before, but under the circumstances, he'd let it sit on his desk.

Abigail read the words on the paper and then with her brows scrunched together she looked up at him.

"I don't know what this is," she whined.

Carson laughed again as he sat down next to her on the floor and took the document from her. "This, my love, is a deed."

"A deed. As in ownership?"

He nodded. "As of yesterday, I own the building your store is in."

Abigail pursed her lips. "So you're going to raise the rent?"

"I hadn't thought of that." He set the papers aside and pulled her to lay down next to him. "You and Clare never have to pay rent again."

Now her eyes went wide. "You bought the building, so we didn't have to pay? Carson…"

"There's more." He brushed a strand of hair back from her face and tucked it behind her ear. "The space next-door is closing shop. I had an architect look at it and we can put a door through from your shop to the one next door."

"To expand?"

"If that's what you girls want to do. But I was also thinking that you could set up all the linens from Mrs. Winters in the next shop. Donna said they have so many."

Abigail pressed her fingertips to her lips. "Oh, Carson. I don't know what to say."

"Say thank you. That's all you ever have to say. I love you, Abi. I'd give you the moon if I could."

She reached for him and rolled him atop of her. "Thank you. I love you, Mr. Stone."

He looked down into her eyes which caught the flicker of flame from the fire. "Oh, future Mrs. Stone, you make me very happy. To think this is the beginning of a very long and happy life, well it makes me optimistically giddy."

"Giddy is very sexy on you," she offered as she began to unbutton his shirt.

"Tell me we're alone. I suddenly am very shy about getting naked on the living room floor with you," he joked as she pulled the shirt from his shoulders.

"Totally alone."

With that promise, he took her mouth with his, and her body with his hands making love to the woman he cherished right there with the fire glow surrounding them. For the moment, they had only one another and no worries of what the darkness had been trying to tell Abigail.

~

ABIGAIL HAD A POT OF COFFEE BREWED AND WARM MUFFINS PLATED on the prep table the moment Clare walked through the door.

"Good, you're here," Clare snarled as she hung up her coat. "I get the next day off."

"You deserve it. How was it with Patricia filling in?"

"It was fine," she said as she pulled down an apron and tied it around her waist. "She has a knack." Clare looked at the set up on the table. "What's all this?"

"Just a little breakfast before we get started." She slid the envelope Carson had given her across the table. "I also wanted to share my Christmas gift with you."

"You're already getting Christmas gifts? How much begging did you have to do for this?"

"None. He wanted to give it to me the other night, but then..."

"Yeah, but then."

"Open it."

Clare lifted the documents out of the envelope and studied it. "Carson bought the building?"

Abigail dropped her shoulders. "I didn't get that at first."

"It says right here," she offered as she pointed to a line in the document.

"Fine. But yes. He bought the building. No more rent."

That had Clare's eyes widening. "No kidding?"

"No kidding. And he's going to have a doorway put through the unit next door, which is leaving, and we can expand our store or continue with the linens."

"The linens are selling like crazy. Both Mrs. Winters' and your mothers."

"I know." She took the papers back from Clare. "It's a pretty great Christmas gift isn't it?"

"You're a very lucky woman." Clare picked up her mug of coffee and took a sip. "Now can we stop beating around the bush? What happened to you the other day?"

She should have known it was coming, Abigail thought. She tucked the deed back into her purse, picked up her coffee, and took a sip. "I think someone is trying to warn me about something."

"Who?"

She winced at the thought of telling her the whole story. "So, it happens that Katie Meadows…"

"The dead girl in Kansas City?"

Abigail winced again at her description. "Yes. Anyway, her great-aunt was Mrs. Winters."

Clare eased her elbows to the table and looked at Abigail. "No kidding."

"I figured that was the connection. Mrs. Winters somehow connected with me so I could find, or because I found, her niece. Anyway, I couldn't sleep that night, after what happened in here. So I was in the living room, and when Carson came out to see me, I saw a spirit."

"Whoa! You saw a ghost?"

"It's not the first."

"Who else?"

Why hadn't she told her any of this? Oh, because it sounded crazy, that's why.

"I saw Mrs. Winters the night she died."

Clare's lips curled into a smile. "That's wicked."

"Don't tease me."

"No teasing. I'm into it. Keep going."

Abigail gave some thought to what she wanted to say. "Anyway, it just so happens that Mrs. Winters' husband was killed in a mine collapse when he was hunting. He and another man both died. The man was Mrs. Winters' brother-in-law, who happens to be Katie Meadows' grandfather."

Clare eased back off her elbows, pulled a chair over, and sat down. "So who came to visit you?"

"Katie Meadows' grandfather. I don't know if he was just there to thank me or if he came with a warning."

"What kind of warning?"

"I don't know." Abigail began pulling the wrapper off of her muffin to give herself a moment to think. "I made Carson kiss me again to see if I'd black out again."

"That was scary."

"I know. He was scared too. But we did it. The same thing happened, only I didn't black out in front of him." Clare's expression had gone blank, so Abigail continued. "I had the same reaction. My head spun, everything went dark, and I couldn't breathe. It was as if something was collapsing around me."

"Like a mine?"

"Maybe. But I didn't pass out. In fact, he didn't even know anything happened."

"You told him, right?"

Abigail shook her head. "No." She held up her hand to stop any harassment headed her way. "I just have to figure out what they're trying to tell me. I don't know if there is something lost in that mine or…"

"You're not going to go digging around and find out."

"No. I just want to know what the darkness is."

Clare reached for Abigail's hands, and she felt the warmth of the touch and complete calm. It was a welcomed feeling.

"I'm here for you. I'll help you any way I can."

"I appreciate that," she said, and she truly did. Family was very important, and she was grateful to have Clare by her side.

CHAPTER 42

*I*t was easy enough to get lost in the holiday spirit, and Abigail embraced it. She and Clare had worked with one of the local high schools to have their choir sing at the store the night before Christmas Eve, while shoppers combed the streets for those last minute gifts and horse-drawn carriages encouraged holiday cheer as they drove patrons up and down the street.

Snow had been promised, and it fell like a soft kiss from Heaven.

Carson slid his arms around Abigail's waist as they watched women fuss over Mrs. Winters' linens.

"I can't see her or feel her, but I can imagine she is among them steering them to certain pieces," Abigail offered.

"It wouldn't surprise me," he agreed. "How much longer are you two going to stay open? It's hours after close."

"But look at all the happy people around. You can't close while they're still around."

He kissed her cheek. "I'm going to head home. I'll have dinner waiting for you when you get there. Don't be too long."

Carson wished he'd given more thought to dinner. He'd have liked to have cooked something fantastic and have it waiting for Abigail when she got home. Looking through the refrigerator, he realized they'd been eating out quite a lot. There were containers of leftovers, but very few fresh ingredients. He moved to the pantry and found a box of spaghetti and can of sauce.

"I guess we're going to wing it," he said to himself as he hummed along with the Christmas song playing through the speakers.

Carson gathered the pots he needed to cook dinner. He filled one with water and started the burner. The tree lights caught his eye as he pulled a can opener from the drawer. Had they been that bright when he'd turned on the tree?

With the can opener still in his hand, he walked out to the living room as the Christmas song that was playing faded and "All Star" by Smash Mouth began. He felt the tears clog in his throat as he listened to Jeffery's favorite song.

"Are you here?" Carson asked, his voice cracking as he did so.

The lights on the tree flickered.

Carson wondered if Jeffery would show himself. He set the can opener on the coffee table and walked toward the stereo to turn down the song which seemed to grow louder.

"What do you think of her Christmas decorating? It doesn't look like your grandmother's house anymore, does it?"

The lights flickered again.

"I miss you like crazy this time of year." The tears that threatened spilled down his cheeks and he wiped them away as quickly as they fell. "Can you believe I got so lucky to find a woman like Abigail?" He laughed at his comment as he raked his fingers through his hair. "I guess I didn't find her at all. Your grandmother delivered me right to her."

The lights flickered again. "I'm so happy, Jeff. You can't imagine."

Carson turned to the stereo when he heard the music change

and resume the Christmas music. The lights on the tree settled back into their normal twinkle, and Carson knew Jeffery's visit was over.

After everything they'd been through the past week, the visit from Jeffery had lightened his spirit. It humored him too. Talking to ghosts wasn't something he ever thought he'd do. Over the past sixteen years, he'd thought of Jeffery every day. He'd done his share of talking to him too, he supposed. He just never thought he'd visit.

Carson understood that he owed Mrs. Winters a great deal. Had Jeffery had something to do with that as well? It seemed like they had as many supporters in the other realm as they did wandering with them on Earth.

He picked up the can opener as he heard a bell ring behind him. When he turned, he noticed the shimmering ornament on the tree, one he hadn't remembered hanging as Abigail gave him direct orders as to where to hang each ornament.

Reaching out, he turned the small bell. Baby's First Christmas 1984.

"Damn, you sure do know how to make an entrance."

As he turned, the bell rang again. Carson glanced at it and then let it ring as he continued to get dinner finished for the woman he loved.

ABIGAIL EMBRACED THE FEELING OF CARSON'S SKIN PRESSED TO hers, his arms wrapped lovingly around her, and his breath soft on her neck. She thought about what he'd told her at dinner, his conversation with Jeffery. He'd shown her the ornament on the tree. Carson had given it a ring, but Abigail chose not to touch it. She wasn't sure who had put it there, but she was sure she understood the full intent of that sign. It had been on her mind a lot lately.

That thought was for a different day. That wasn't going to cloud her mind at the moment. For now, she was going to enjoy the soft sound of the wind bringing snow in for Christmas, and the heat blowing through the vent. If everything fell right into place, she and Carson were going to have the most spectacular Christmas morning. That much she knew. But for now, she would let herself fall asleep in his arms, just as she wanted to every night for the rest of her life.

∾

CARSON WOKE WITH A START WHEN HIS PHONE BUZZED ON THE nightstand next to him. He quickly reached for it, noting that the clock said three-thirty. The number on the display wasn't one he recognized, but it was local. Looking next to him, he realized that Abigail hadn't heard the phone. Jumping from the bed, he hurried toward the other room to answer the phone.

The voice on the other end identified themselves as police. It seemed as though somebody had broken in the back door of the building he had just purchased. The building of the tea shop.

He had confirmed that they had not done any destruction to the tea shop itself. The unit next door, they said, might have had some damage. It looked like his Christmas Eve morning was about to start off very early.

Carson went back to the bedroom quietly. He slipped on his clothes and skirted the bed to Abigail's side. Gently, he rested a hand on her bare arm.

"Abi, I have to run into town. I'll be right back."

She stirred, nodded her head, but never opened her eyes.

Carson bent down and kissed her on the forehead. He made sure to leave a note as well. It was obvious she wasn't hearing him at all.

Maybe, he could be back in bed, wrapped in her arms, before she ever woke up.

The snow which had fallen the night before shimmered under the streetlights. Carson pulled up to the building he'd owned for a few weeks and parked next to the police cruisers. He could see that the door to the store next to the tea shop had been kicked in. One of the officers escorted him inside to look around.

It looked as if perhaps someone had broken in to stay out of the cold. Other than the back door, nothing looked to have been tampered with. With the officer still at his side, he unlocked the door to the tea shop and walked in. Behind them, the door slammed shut.

"That's a tricky door," the officer said.

"I'll want to give that a look. I don't remember it doing that before. Certainly don't want somebody getting hurt."

They walked through the kitchen and checked the storage room. Nothing seemed out of the ordinary, until the water in the sink began to run.

Carson noted that the officer had his hand on the butt of his gun.

He moved to the sink and turned off the water. "Old buildings are funny, aren't they?"

"I don't know why people want to preserve these old buildings," the officer said as he looked around skeptically. "It makes sense to me to tear down old buildings and build sturdy ones. After all, what does it take to heat this place? It's freezing in here."

For a moment, Carson wanted to pat the officer on the back. Finally, somebody understood that not all old buildings should remain standing. However, the fact that he could see his breath inside the tea shop made him nervous. Neither Abigail nor Clare had mentioned anything about the heat. It was going to cost double to have somebody come out and look at it, but he didn't want the pipes to freeze that was for sure.

"I don't see any damage in here. It looks like somebody was looking for a place to stay for the night. I don't expect we'll have much more of a problem with that. The space next door will be renovated the first part of the year."

The officer gave him a nod. "We will make sure to keep an eye on it the next few nights. Usually, things are pretty calm around Christmas."

"I think I'll be okay here. I want to look at the furnace if you want to take off."

"Have a Merry Christmas," the officer said.

"Merry Christmas."

Carson waited for the officer to walk out of the shop, and the door closed quietly behind him, but he heard the lock engage. A moment later, he felt the warmth fill the air as the heater kicked on in the tea shop.

A month ago he would have already been on the phone finding somebody to fix the situation. But now, he was fairly sure someone was messing with him. Someone he loved, who wasn't living.

*a*s Carson stood alone in the store, the lights came on.

"I'm not sure what's going on, but cut it out," he said in the empty store, his voice echoing against the walls. "Do you need me here?"

As if in reply, the lights turned off.

"Did someone break in?"

The lights turned back on, and he assumed he had his answer.

"The police are going to watch the place. I think someone was just cold. Everything's okay."

The lights fluttered and then turned off.

Since he seemed to have the system of talking to them, whoever they were, he thought he ask a few more questions.

"Mr. Mason, is that you?"

The shop remained dark and quiet.

"Jeffery? Are you here?"

Still, the shop remained dark.

Carson took a deep breath. "Mrs. Winters?"

The light slowly lifted.

Carson smiled. "It's nice to have you visit. It's a bit early in the day for a visit though. Perhaps we can catch up at another time."

Lights dim begin then quickly came back up. He heard the door rattle, and the lock open. Then, the lights went out.

He wasn't sure if he upset her, but he assumed that she'd visit again. But just as he moved to the door and grasped the handle, the door locked again.

"I thought we were done here. Are you trying to keep me here?"

The lights came on and grew brighter. He suddenly felt a drop in the temperature again. The water in the kitchen came on again.

"I don't know what you're doing." He hurried back to the kitchen to turn off the water.

He assumed he was communicating with Mrs. Winters. However, she'd never been devious like this. Did death do this to a person?

The temperature in the kitchen was even colder than the other room. Again, Carson could see his breath. The frost had formed on the window which looked out over the parking lot in the back of the building.

"My pipes are going to break. Do you need to make it this cold?"

It was then he noticed letters appearing in the frost. His heart began to race. Perhaps he was actually asleep, he thought. Nothing like this had ever happened before. He felt as though he had stepped right out of a horror movie, though he knew the spirit with him was kind.

Carson moved toward the window as the words formed: go home.

He repeated the words softly. The lights in the kitchen came on, and the air warmed. "Okay, I'll go home." He felt as though Mrs. Winters' message had gotten through, then a panic burst in his chest. "Is Abigail okay?"

He notice that the temperature gone to normal, and the words faded from the window. The lights in the kitchen turned off and the lock on the front door released.

Perhaps Mrs. Winters just wanted him back home with his fiancée. Of course, that's where he wanted to be anyway.

Carson moved swiftly through the shop, letting himself out the front door, and locking it behind him. What a strange morning.

A moment later he was in his car, with the engine on, thankful for heated seats. It was now only four-thirty and still dark as night. If he were lucky, Abigail would still be sleeping. Nothing sounded better than curling up next to her warm body.

Carson drove out of the lot, stopping before he headed out onto Washington Street. He sat at the stop sign for a moment. It would be a prime opportunity to check on their rental properties, he mused to himself. Who would have thought in a few short months he'd have finished his house, rented it, gotten engaged, rented her house, and moved into Mrs. Winters' house. When he thought of the whirlwind that had been his life since September, it amused him. He also realized, he'd never been so happy in his entire life. And with all that happiness, now he was talking to ghosts too. The thought made him laugh out loud.

What the heck, he thought. He'd drive over to Abigail's house and just pass by, making sure everything looked okay. As he did so, he'd pass right by the Ford Street church project on his way north to his rental. He'd hit Highway 93 back out, and still be home before five o'clock.

Carson turned right onto Washington and navigated toward Abigail's house which they had quickly rented. As he passed by, he could see the light was on over the sink in the kitchen. For some reason, that sign in a house would always make him think of his mother. Before bed each night, she would turn on the light over the sink. It was comforting.

Making his way back to Ford Street, he felt the car chill, and the radio turned up. Again, playing one of Jeffery's favorite songs.

"Seriously, man. While I'm driving isn't the best time for you to visit."

He wondered if he would soon be seeing them, just as Abigail did. Was this what touching her had done to him? Would their children be clairvoyant too?

Carson turned down the radio and increased the temperature in the car. As he pulled out onto Ford Street, the church came into view. He slowed as he passed in front of the structure, now only bare outer walls. The gates were still in place to keep people out, but it was then he noticed the flicker of light coming from the back of the church. Was that fire?

He eased the car to a stop.

Someone had a fire in a trashcan in the corner of the church. They didn't have a big homeless population, so why was it that everyone was breaking into his properties tonight, he wondered.

Carson put the car in park, which unlocked his door. As he unbuckled his seatbelt, the door locked again. He unlocked it, and it locked again.

"Dude! Quit messing with me," he said as the radio turned up louder.

Carson turned off the radio again and unlocked the door. "Leave me alone for today, okay? I have things I have to attend to."

This time the door opened and Carson stepped out onto the frozen earth. "Hey," he shouted down into the structure. "You can't be in there."

He saw the figure of a person bundle tighter under a blanket by the makeshift fire.

"Seriously, man. You have to go," he shouted again. The person inside didn't budge.

Carson dug his keys out of his pocket and unlocked the gate. He wasn't about abandoning the person in the cold, but he needed to get them to safety.

Walking around the outside of the building, he could see the person by the fire. Was that a dog or a child bundled in the blanket with them?

"Hey, I'm here to get you somewhere safe. This building isn't safe right now," he said as he eased himself over the small wall that let him into the side of the building. "We need to put out that fire. Seriously, man, this is bad. I'd be happy to take you to a shelter."

The person in the blanket stood, and the dog which had been under there with him ran into the dark of the building.

Crap, Carson thought. He reached into his pocket for his phone to call for help, only to realize he'd left it in the car. He'd try to talk the man—he could now see it was for sure a man—out once more before turning it over to the authorities.

"My name is Carson. I own this building. We are working on restoring it. There might be chemicals that shouldn't be around fire. Why don't you come with me? I'll get you somewhere warm," he shouted toward the man.

The man shook his head, and it was then Carson heard the dog, and another voice from behind him. In fact, there were many voices. Seriously, didn't these people have shelters they could go to? It was Christmas Eve. No one deserved to be out in the cold and snow on Christmas Eve.

The person coming toward him was a woman, and she had a child at her side.

"He's deaf. He doesn't talk to many people."

"Listen, we need to get you all out of here. I'll make sure you get somewhere warm with food." He'd take them back to the tea shop if he had to. "This building is not stable enough for people to be building fires in it or in here without a hard hat."

"You can get us shelter?" the woman asked.

"I can."

Carson felt the wind begin to kick up through the support braces. Wind, cold, and fire didn't make him very comfortable standing within the fragile walls of the church.

"My car is on the street. How many of you are there?"

"There are four of us," she said as she pushed the child toward him. "Take her. I have my son and my mother. I'll get them."

Carson picked up the little girl and hurried back to the wall. He managed to carry her out of the structure and to his car. "I'll turn this on, and it'll keep you warm," he offered, setting her in the back seat.

He went back to the entrance where the woman lifted a young boy of maybe two-years-old to him. Carson repeated the process with the boy and went back to the others.

The woman was trying to push her mother over the wall when the wind picked up and blew in a freezing ice. The older woman fell back to the ground.

"I can't get her. She's too frail."

Carson jumped down into the church and picked up the older woman. "You go ahead of us. The kids are in the car with the heater on. I'll carry her around," he said.

The woman hurried off toward the street.

"We're going to get you somewhere warm," he promised the woman as he walked under the structure he could hear swaying above him. The man continued to watch as Carson managed to climb out of the church on a dirt ramp that the crew had put in.

He was exhausted and frozen to the bone by the time he got the woman to the car.

The wind had kicked up harder by then and the cold burned through him. "Do you know the man still in there?"

"He showed us to the church, but that's all. I don't know him."

"I'm going to go try one more time to get him out."

CHAPTER 44

*A*bigail pulled the comforter up closer to her chin. The house seemed to have gotten much colder. Perhaps the snow was piling up outside. What a wonderful Christmas Eve, she thought.

The room was still dark. She kept her eyes closed willing herself back to sleep. The room grew even colder, and she swore she could hear the faint sound of a bell.

She tried to open her eyes, but she just couldn't. The sound of the bell grew louder. She moved her arm to feel for Carson, but he wasn't there.

The sound of the bell grew louder still, and her eyes remained closed.

Abigail began to cough. The air had gotten thick with dust.

She tried to move through the darkness, but her body was constricted within the sheet. Her arms were pinned to her side, and she gasped for air.

Her head swam, just as it had when she blacked out from kissing Carson. But this time she was fully awake, but her eyes still wouldn't open.

There was a light, in the corner of the room she was standing.

A fire? The sun? Dust kicked up around her and caused her to cough again, only this time her eyes flew open, and the sound of the bell became her telephone.

She picked it up to answer, but there was no one on the other end.

The room had gotten colder.

Abigail fought her way out of the sheets and pulled on the first clothes she found on the floor. With her phone in her hand, she headed to the kitchen. There she found a note from Carson. *Have gone to the new building—your building. Police called. 3:30 AM. I love you. C.*

Abigail looked at the clock on the microwave. It was already five-forty-five.

She pressed the button on her phone to call Carson, but it went directly to voicemail. Standing in the kitchen alone, she heard the bell again.

The air around her head had cooled so much she could see her breath. Hurrying out to the Christmas tree she watched as the baby's first Christmas bell continue to chime.

She wasn't sure who was with her, but she knew somebody was there.

"Is Carson in trouble?"

The bell rang again as if somebody were madly shaking it.

Abigail ran back to the kitchen, pulled her keys from her purse, and grabbed a coat as she ran for her car. She slid on the fresh snow, tumbling to the ground. Her elbow and her butt throbbed from the landing.

Sitting in the snow on the driveway, she pressed a hand to her stomach. She thought she might be sick.

The bell on the tree hadn't been quite a surprise to her. Unconfirmed, but not a surprise. She was sure that's why the fear that swirled inside of her threatened to debilitate her.

Willing herself to her feet, she opened the car door and climbed inside.

She started the engine and warmth from the heater immediately filled the car. Without her companion, whom she couldn't see, she was sure it would've been a cold drive into town.

She headed toward the empty highway and wondered if she should call somebody. Unfortunately, she didn't know who to call or where to send them.

She was headed toward her store, which was the last place she'd known him to be.

～

CARSON HAD HEARD THE SCREAM AND HURRIED BACK TO HELP THE man out of the church. As he'd gone over the wall, and down into the church, he heard the creaking sounds around him as the wind kicked up.

It was then he noticed the can that had held the fire had blown over and the blanket around the man had caught fire. The man flailed, whipping flames into the air.

Carson moved in swiftly to pull the man to the ground. With his body on top of the other man's he rolled them across the snow-laden ground as another gust of wind blew through the structure, and the first beam crashed to the ground.

～

ABIGAIL DROVE PAST THE TEA SHOP, BUT CARSON'S CAR WASN'T there. She saw the tire tracks in the snow from the cars that must have been there earlier. Perhaps she'd passed him on the way home, but whichever spirit had been with her told her he was in trouble.

As she pulled back out to Washington, the sun now just peeking through the trees, she turned her car toward Ford Street as if compelled to go to the construction site.

From just beyond the church, she saw a fire truck racing toward the scene, as well as an ambulance.

Carson's car was on the street, the lights and engine were on, and she could see people inside.

She pulled up behind his car as a woman got out and went to her. "The man is in the building," she said as her voice shook. "He went after the other man."

Abigail started toward the fence, but a police officer stepped in front of her.

"You can't go in there," he said as he held up his hand. "The structure is unstable with this wind."

"My fiancée is in there." She reached for the gate, but the officer blocked her entrance.

Abigail looked past him to where the firefighters lowered themselves into the building. Pain ripped through her chest when she saw three forms near where the firefighters moved to. Clearly, she knew they were Mrs. Winters, Jeffery, and Justice.

The officer moved in front of her and grabbed her arms. She looked into his eyes as the blackness took over, and her knees buckled, taking her and the officer to the ground.

CHAPTER 45

*A*bigail could hear the voice calling her name, but again her eyes wouldn't open. Was she asleep? Her body felt heavy.

"Abigail," the voice said again, only now her ears seemed clearer, and she could hear the voice. Her mother? No. His mother. Patricia's voice was the voice she heard.

"There's our girl," Patricia said as Abigail's eyes finally opened to see her standing over her. His father was there, too. Patricia's hands moved to her mouth, and then she wiped away a tear. "Oh, honey. Thank goodness you're okay. You had us worried sick."

Abigail moved her arm to push herself up, but something dangled from it. A wire?

It was then she realized she was in a hospital room. Her head throbbed, and she pressed her hand to her forehead. "Where am I?"

"In the hospital, honey. You hit your head when you fell. The police officer tried to catch you, but you both went down. You've been out for a few hours now."

Abigail worked to sit up in the bed, and Patricia reached for her to help her. She felt her touch, but there was no energy between them. "What are they giving me?"

"Fluids. You're dehydrated. It happens," Patricia said with a smile as she stepped back and Al wrapped an arm around his wife's shoulders.

Abigail felt the tears stinging her eyes. Why else would Carson's parents be standing with her and not with him? They would only be there if Carson hadn't made it.

The very thought had the tears rolling down her cheeks.

"Oh, honey. Are you in pain?" Patricia turned toward Al. "Get someone for her."

"No. No." She wiped at her cheeks. "I'm fine."

She took a moment to catch her breath.

Patricia moved to the table beside the bed and picked up a glass of water with a straw. "Why don't you sip this. They want you to keep calm and stay hydrated. You have to take care of yourself. We don't want anything to happen to the baby and…"

Patricia stopped talking when Abigail gasped. She felt her jaw drop as she stared at Patricia.

"I've said too much." Patricia set the glass back down and moved next to her husband again. "I'm so sorry. They took your blood work, and well, they assumed we knew, and they didn't want to give you the wrong medicine, and…"

"Baby?" Abigail heard the word come from her, but she was too stunned to actually know she'd said it.

"Yes. You didn't know?"

She moved her hand to her stomach and felt the energy she'd felt yesterday before the ornament arrived on the tree. "I only thought that maybe…"

"We're thrilled," Patricia assured her as she reached for her, and again Abigail only felt the touch, no energy from her. "It's a Christmas miracle, right?" She looked up at Al for his say.

"A miracle," he agreed.

Abigail rested back on the bed. Why would they call it a miracle? She winced when she thought about the spirits that had been standing around Carson in the building.

She squeezed her eyes closed and fought back the tears, and the sobbing she knew was coming again. There was only one reason for them to assume the baby was a miracle, and that was if the spirits were there to take Carson with them.

When she felt as though she could control her emotions enough to talk to his parents, Abigail opened her eyes.

Both Patricia and Al stood there watching her.

"The building collapsed, didn't it? He was trying to save the building instead of tearing it down. It collapsed."

Carson's parents exchanged looks. "Yes," Patricia said. "There was a fire from a vagrant, and the wind blew through and beams fell."

Abigail thought of the visions she'd had. The dust in her lungs. The darkness. It hadn't been the men in the mine at all. It had been Carson.

The tears came again, and every inch of her body ached.

"Oh, honey. It's okay. Be calm for the baby," Patricia begged, but Abigail couldn't calm down now. She hadn't known she was going to fall in love with the man when she'd met him—or she hadn't wanted to—but now how would she live without him?

The door to the room opened, and a nurse stepped in. "Mr. And Mrs. Stone, he's out now," she said.

Patricia thanked her before turning back to Abigail.

She sat up, wiping away the tears with the sheet. "Who's out? Out of where?"

Patricia took her hand and held it. "Carson is out of surgery."

"He's alive?"

"Of course he is."

Abigail's breath came quicker as the tears dried. "But Mrs. Winters, Jeffery, and Justice were there. They were with him."

Patricia smiled as if she thought Abigail was crazy. "Well, maybe they were there to protect him. He has a few burns on his chest and arms from helping that man who was in the church. But the man survived too, thanks to Carson. He also has a few broken bones, but he should be healed before the wedding."

"He's alive?"

Now Patricia's eyes welled with tears as she laughed through them. "Yes, dear. He's alive and will be thrilled to hear about the baby."

"He doesn't know?"

"Only we know."

And Jeffery, Abigail thought. "Don't say anything. I want to tell him."

Patricia patted Abigail's hand. "You get some rest. We're going to see him. He'll be spending Christmas here this year, but we can all gather in his room."

Abigail watched as they left her room. Carson was okay, she thought, and the tears returned as happy tears.

She touched her stomach and felt the energy connect to the baby that she and Carson had made. "I knew you were in there. I just knew. You saved your daddy, didn't you? You sent everyone to protect him."

It would be months before she could feel the life that grew inside of her, but she knew the energy. This baby would work miracles. She had no doubt that Mrs. Winters had picked this baby for them.

CHAPTER 46

They kept Abigail under observation for a few more hours, but when they were ready to release her, Patricia came for her.

"Are you alright to walk?" she asked as Abigail stood next to the bed.

"I'm fine. I just want to go to him."

Patricia nodded. "He looks bad, Abi. I don't want to sugarcoat it. He's bandaged up because of the burns. But really, the burns aren't as bad as we had first thought. His leg is bad, but they went in and fixed what they could. There will be more surgeries to come, but..."

Abigail reached out to touch her arm, enjoying that there was only peace when she did so. "I don't care how he looks. I love your son, and nothing will stop me from continuing to love him."

Patricia smiled through the sadness she wore on her face. "He loves you, Abi. We love you too. You're the perfect addition to this family."

She pulled Abigail in close and held her.

"I'm ready to see him."

Patricia nodded and led her out of the room.

CARSON HATED MEDICATIONS. HE HATED HOSPITALS. HE HATED not being able to get up out of the damn bed and walk around the room. Every part of his body was bandaged and ached. What the hell had he gone to the church for? Had he just gone back home, he'd be with Abigail and not in this stupid hospital room.

The moment the door to the room opened he was ready to let his anger fly at the person who walked in. He wanted comfort, food, more painkillers.

But when he saw his lovely bride-to-be walk in on the arm of his mother, his emotions flipped on him, and tears streamed down his cheeks instead.

"God, Abi, I'm so happy to see you." He wept as she moved toward him.

"How do you feel?"

"Horrible. This medication is making me sick."

She smiled at him as if she understood. "I understand. It does that to me, too."

"I look horrible, don't I?" he asked and turned his head from her.

"You look like a hero, Carson. You saved an entire family. I'm so proud of you."

"I'll be scarred."

"Really? You're worried about that? I'm not. I love you."

He reached for her with the hand he had free, and she took it.

"You're going to be okay," she said, with relief coloring her face. "I can see it. You're going to be okay very soon."

Through the tears, he laughed. "You know one thing I've learned in our short time together? You can't read me. You're full of crap."

The pink in her cheeks grew even rosier, and she laughed, as did his mother who stepped up next to the bed. "Your father and I are going to go home for a bit and gather some things. We will be back. This isn't going to stop our Christmas traditions." Patricia blew him a kiss and left the room.

"I'm sorry you were woken up like this. That had to have been a horrible call."

Abigail bit down on her lip as she carefully sat on the edge of the bed, still holding his hand. "I didn't get a call. I was there, Carson. I saw you."

It hurt to turn his head, but he met her eye. "You were there? How could you have…"

"They let me know."

"They—oh," he eased into the pillow behind him. "How?"

"That was the darkness I kept seeing when I'd touch you. They were telling me to keep you safe. Then that bell on the tree kept ringing. It was enough to pull me out of bed. I saw your note, and I headed into town."

Carson closed his eyes for a moment as he felt the calm of the medicine pump into his veins from the machine at his side. "They were with me," he said as he opened his eyes and looked at her again. "Someone locked me in the tea shop, and even told me to go home." He chuckled when he thought of it, then winced when it caused him pain. "I should have gone home."

"I saw them over you at the construction site. I thought they'd come to take you. Oh, Carson, I was so afraid."

"I will never leave you, Abi. I love you so much I would never go without a fight."

"Well, now I know, they'll never let you pass over without one too."

Carson studied her, still in her pajamas, and it had to be late afternoon. He noticed the band on her arm and the tape. "Why are you wearing hospital bands?"

She looked at her wrist and smiled. "I seem to have blacked out when I saw our friends around you, and I hit my head. I was out for a few hours your mother said. They gave me fluids and let me rest. I'm okay now. I just have a bump on my head."

"Abi, I'm so sorry."

"Never be sorry."

Carson wished he could shift in bed and hold her. There was nothing he wanted more than to be able to wrap his arms around her. He realized that he was grateful to be able to hold her again. Without guardian angels all around him, he might have been without her—or more likely—her without him, forever.

"The bell on the tree woke you up?"

She nodded. "As if someone were trying to break it."

"Who do you think put that bell there? I didn't do it. And it rang last night when Jeffery was there."

Abigail smiled. "I think it was Jeffery that put it there. It was his bell."

"Of all the ornaments he could have chosen, that one was funny, don't you think?"

"No, I don't think it was funny at all. In fact, it was the perfect gift to accompany my Christmas gift."

Carson licked his lips as his mouth had suddenly gone dry. "I don't understand. You planned that with Jeffery?"

She laughed, and the sound eased his pains. "No. He just knew." The pink of her cheeks deepened again. "See I had this feeling, well, I think I was hoping…" She took a deep breath and pressed her free hand to her chest. "We're going to have a baby, Carson."

Carson stared at her. He damned the moment not being able to sit up and hold her, but her eyes lit with that warmth. How could he possibly be sad or upset? She still loved him, that was evident in how she looked at him all battered and bruised. And they were going to have a baby.

A baby!

"Abi, I never thought in my life that I'd want that as much as I do. You're sure?"

She nodded. "Your mother told me. They took blood when I came in and…"

"You're pregnant."

"I am."

The laugh broke through the haze that the medicine was causing. "My mother knew first?"

"She did."

"We are never going to live that down."

"Oh, but Carson, we knew months ago. I knew the moment I met you. In fact, after you and Mrs. Winters left my store I went into the kitchen and told Clare you were the man I was going to marry."

"You didn't even like me."

"I didn't want to like you." She moved to kiss the top of his head. "I couldn't help but love you though."

"I still promise to make you very happy," he said, and he heard his words slur. "All of you. You and all of our babies."

Abigail let out a sigh. "I have no doubt you'll walk the straight and narrow there. Mrs. Winters will see to that."

As he felt his eyes begin to shut and the medicine started to take him under he heard Mrs. Winters' voice as clearly as if she were standing there. "Merry Christmas, Carson."

EPILOGUE

*A*s far as hospital stays went, Abigail thought she had it best. Flowers decorated her room. Cards lined the window sill. Her baby girl slept in the bassinet to her side.

She'd managed a comb through her hair and nursed the baby before she received Carson's phone call that he was on his way up.

The anticipation of the visit filled her with joy. She couldn't wait for the door to open.

As she waited, she noticed a shimmering in the corner of the room. She'd become accustomed to it nearly everywhere she went. If it wasn't Mrs. Winters keeping an eye on her, it was her grandmother. It seemed in the afterlife they had become quite close.

When the door opened, Abigail felt the joy in her heart nearly burst through in her smile.

She watched her family walk into the room.

"Good morning, Ellie and Jeffery." She shifted to look at the little boy hoisted on Carson's hip. "And good morning my sweet Justice. Are you awake?"

The toddler rested his head on Carson's shoulder.

"Can we see her, mama?" Ellie's sweet voice filled Abigail's heart.

"Of course you can. Why don't you all come up here with me?"

Ellie, now a beautiful five-year-old with pigtails of spun gold, climbed up on the bed, kissing Abigail on the cheek before taking a seat. Jeffery, the toughest three-year-old ever, pulled himself up until he, too, could take a seat on the bed.

Carson handed the nearly two-year-old Justice to her, and she held him against her, just as Carson had.

They'd been through the process enough times to know Justice would be the least interested in seeing the baby. That would change though. In time they would be the best of friends.

Carson walked to the bassinet and lifted out the tiny bundle wrapped in pink. He pressed a kiss to the forehead of the newest member of the Stone family.

"Okay, guys. Mommy and I want you to meet your new sister. This is Gwendolyn."

Ellie's face lit up, and the smile grew wide. "Just like great-grandma?"

Abigail nodded. "Just like great-grandma. Does she still visit you?"

Ellie also nodded. "Yes. She's very happy that we have a new sister."

Abigail exchanged glances with Carson. Thank goodness he was open-minded. Ellie had been talking about her friend Mrs. Winters, whom she knew she was named after, and her great-grandmother since she could talk.

Jeffery leaned in and looked at her. "She looks weird."

Abigail laughed. "All babies are a little weird looking. You were too."

That seemed to roll right off of him as soon as their sister stretched and opened her eyes.

Abigail saw the connection the moment it happened. She wondered if Carson saw it too. It was as if Gwendolyn made contact with her brother and sister, and even Justice who turned to look at her. They were a unit. They belonged together, just as Carson and Abigail had belonged together.

CARSON SAT DOWN ON THE BED NEXT TO HIS WIFE, HIS NEW daughter in his arms. Their children moved in to see her, and Abigail rested her head on his shoulder.

That afternoon nearly six years ago when Mrs. Winters changed their lunch plans, he never would have guessed it would have changed his life. Luckily he had the opportunity to thank her every day, as he knew she still hung around the house.

"We sure do have a perfect life, don't we?" Abigail whispered as they watched their family bond with the newest member.

"I didn't know this was what I wanted. I'm sure glad it was fated for us."

"Lucky for us, we had someone to lead the way."

We hope you enjoyed Bernadette Marie's *The Tea Shop.*

Here is an excerpt from one of her Romantic Suspense novels, Chasing Shadows.

CHASING SHADOWS

*I*cy fingers of cold air pressed against Declan Matthews' shirt as the wind blew through the trees. Once upon a time the wooded area, less than a mile from his childhood home, would have been a place of refuge. Now it was tainted with death.

The massive tree, which had been brought down by lightning at least fifty years earlier, still made for a perfect bridge over the cold brook that calmly passed beneath it.

It was there that they had found his sister. She had died on that bridge of nature, right where she'd once played as a child.

He heard the footsteps on the dry leaves behind him, but he didn't turn. There was no reason to.

Vaughn moved in beside him, just as an old friend would do, without a word.

They'd shared many hours together in this spot. It was more than a tree in the woods. It had been a pirate ship, a lunar landing site, and a jungle with man-eating monkeys. It had also been a place to camp and have long talks. Or when they'd gotten older, a place to sneak off with one of their dads' beers and a cigar. He'd brought Lacy Pratt out to the log once for a massive make out session, which ended successfully in his car later that night. Of course, that would only be the beginning of the women who refused to talk to him after a relationship ended.

Vaughn shoved his hands into the front pockets of his jeans and rocked back on his heels. "Christ, Declan. I don't even know what to say."

"There's nothing to say."

"I can't believe something like this would happen here. Everyone knows everyone. Who could have done this?"

Declan hated the small town mentality, even if the town was no longer small, as it had been in his early youth. Small was why he'd moved so far away. Ask anyone in a small town who could have done something like murder a married mother of two, and they'd tell you no one. Give them a name and they'd give you a million reasons that person was a saint. He appreciated living in a big city where everyone was guilty of something. He was a lawyer, so he knew what he was talking about. He'd put enough deadbeats away for a long time.

He clenched his fists to his side. "People talk, V. Someone will spill and I'll see them hang for it," he said through gritted teeth. And he meant it. He'd found great restraint in his job, but this wasn't part of his job. This was his little sister, and he'd take revenge if it meant finding the bastard that left her on that log, dead.

"Am I going to have to put a watch on you, Matthews?" The voice came from behind them and both men turned.

Of all people, Lacy Pratt moved toward them. A badge hung around her neck and a gun was holstered on her hip. She looked as if she'd walked out of a detective show on TV in her black slacks and starched white shirt. Her long locks, which he'd once tangled his fingers in, had been traded for a shorter cut that didn't quite hit her shoulders.

As she moved closer, she tucked her hair behind her ear.

"I'm really sorry about what happened. Stacy was a vital part of our community and a good friend," she said, her eyes locked on his.

He realized these were the first words she'd spoken to him in fifteen years. What a crappy thing to have to say.

"Thanks. What's all this?" He nodded toward her badge and she looked down.

"Detective Pratt. I'm working the case."

He felt those icy cold fingers on his back again, but this time the sharpness dug into his skin.

"How long have you been a detective?"

Lacy inched closer, her hands on her hips. "You got a problem with me and this case?"

"I have a problem with this case for sure." He mimicked her stance. "But I don't think that's what I asked. I asked you how long you've been a detective."

He saw the shift in her demeanor as her eyes softened. "Eight years."

"Are you good at your job?"

Her eyes narrowed. "Damn good."

"I'm glad to hear that. I want the S.O.B. caught and I want him to pay."

"We're doing everything we can to…"

"I want more. Someone killed my sister. That's not just something I'm going to forget very quickly. Not only that, they killed her five miles from her house and a mile from where she grew up. And why here? Why did they bring her here?"

Lacy turned to Vaughn. "Give us a minute, will ya?"

Vaughn exchanged looks with Declan, to which Declan gave him a nod to do as she'd asked. He was well aware of the others patrolling around the woods looking for anything that would tie someone to his sister's death. He sure as hell hoped they'd find something.

"Do you have any leads?" he asked looking toward the log

which he thought he might cut into fire wood and burn out of the sheer necessity of making it go away.

"Every single person around is a suspect at this point."

He shifted his glance to look at her standing next to him. He'd admit, for five-three, she was as intimidating as hell with her stance and gun.

"So you've begun questioning everyone?"

"We're doing our job, Matthews."

The last name thing wasn't sitting well with him. "Did you forget my first name?"

"I tried to forget everything about you, but here you are."

He let the stab at him sting as it was meant to. "Well, I'm here now. And I want to know what we're going to do."

"We're going to do our jobs and you're going to let us."

Declan ran his tongue over his teeth. "Get on it then. My family needs some closure."

Lacy pulled her phone from her pocket. "I have some questions for you. I'm going to record our conversation. You got a problem with it?"

"Ask away," he said, facing her and crossing his arms in front of him.

She pushed the button on her phone and then looked up at him. "Where were you yesterday at approximately four-thirty in the afternoon?"

Declan felt himself wince, and when he looked at her, he knew she'd caught that. What the hell did he have to lose?

"I was with my divorce lawyer."

The flash of amusement that lit in her eyes was hard to miss, but she kept her demeanor. "I'll need the name and location of the lawyer and the meeting."

"Fine."

"Divorced, huh? Sucks."

"Tell me about it. Since I've gone there, I've been divorced for two years now. But is seems my ex-wife thinks I withheld income stats from them and she'd like a little more of my hard-earned money. Let me also put out there that I actually walked in on her in my bed with her ex-husband whom she's planning on remarrying."

"Ouch. Kick to the balls, huh?"

"Exactly."

"Can't imagine you'd lie about that, but I still have to check it out."

"I'd expect you to be thorough." Declan dropped his arms and shoved his hands into his pockets. "I took the first flight out of New York this morning. There'll be a paper trail for you too."

"Good to know."

"I haven't been to see my parents yet. I came right here," he admitted. "Have you seen them?"

Her expression softened. "They're devastated."

"Of course."

"Your mom began to clean the house and your dad, well, I don't know how many shots he had."

"What about Tom?"

Lacy tucked her phone back into her pocket. "Yeah, we talked to him. I've been at this a long time, and I've never seen a man as big as him break down as he did. One of those things that'll stick with me."

"Genuine shock?"

She nodded. "Yeah. I suggested maybe he should even go to the hospital. But he refused."

"The kids?"

"They were sleeping by the time we got to him. The department sent counselors over this morning to be there."

Declan pinched the bridge of his nose as a headache began to creep in. "They don't deserve this. No one deserves to live without their mother."

Lacy reached out and touched his arm. "I know how it feels. They'll be okay, but they'll never forget."

Declan lifted his gaze. "I forgot you grew up without your mother. I'm sorry."

"It's why I do what I do. There's a lot of sick people out there, Matthews. I'm here to stop them, and someday no kid will lose their mother like this."

"Maybe you should have gone to talk to my niece and nephew."

She tucked a fallen strand of hair behind her other ear. "If they need me I'll be there. They're good kids."

He nodded in agreement. "I should head to my parents' house. What happens now?"

She expelled a long breath. "We will need someone to positively identify her."

Declan squeezed his eyes closed then opened them slowly. "You really need that?"

"I'm afraid so. Tom said he'd do it, but…"

"I'll do it," he offered. "Dear God, never thought it would be something I'd do, but I'll do it."

Lacy pulled her card from her pocket and handed it to him. "Go to your folks and get settled in. I can meet you in town when you're ready."

He looked down at the Rolex on his wrist, which once was a big deal and now meant crap to him in the scheme of things. "I'll meet you there at three?"

"I'll be there," she confirmed. "Give my condolences to your family."

"I will."

She hesitated for a moment, then shot him a sympathetic smile before she left him alone again with the cold blowing through the trees.

ABOUT THE AUTHOR

Bestselling Author Bernadette Marie is known for building families readers want to be part of. Her series *The Keller Family* has graced bestseller charts since its release in 2011. Since then she has authored and published over thirty books. The married mother of five sons promises romances with a *Happily Ever After always...*and says she can write it because she lives it.

Obsessed with writing since the age of 12, Bernadette Marie officially started her journey as an author in 2007 when she finalized a manuscript she'd been writing for 22 years, shelved it, and wrote 12 more books that year. In 2009 she was contracted with a small publisher in a deal that would eventually go bad. From that experience, she knew she could take control of her career and that's what she did.

A chronic entrepreneur since opening her first salon at the age of twenty, Bernadette Marie established her own publishing house in 2011, *5 Prince Publishing,* so that she could publish the books she liked to write and help make the dreams of other aspiring authors come true too. Believing there is a place for the fresh author's voice, she not only publishes but coaches others who wish to publish their work independently. Bernadette Marie is also the CEO of *Illumination Author Events and Services* offering smaller intimate author/reader events as well as author services. A member of the Rocky Mountain Fiction Writers, she was a finalist for the 2017 Writer of the Year. Bernadette Marie also writes about her journey into parenting 5 teenage boys on her blog and podcast *ThisHouseofBoys.com.*

For more information
www.bernadettemarie.com
info@bernadettemarie.com

OTHER TITLES FROM

 5 PRINCE PUBLISHING

www.5princebooks.com

The Three Stones of Bethany *April Marcom*
Wanderlust *Bernadette Marie*
Holiday Past *Jessica Dall*
Christmas Blitz *Amy Gale*
A Christmas for Chloe *Susan Lohrer*
Restored Hearts *Railyn Stone*
Last Christmas *Lisa J. Hobman*
A Romance for Christmas *Bernadette Marie*
The Fall of Undal *Katrina Sisowath*